ABE LINCOLN
—FOR—
CLASS PRESIDENT!

Other Books by Todd Strasser

ABE LINCOLN FOR CLASS PRESIDENT!

Todd Strasser

AN
APPLE
PAPERBACK

SCHOLASTIC INC.
New York Toronto London Auckland Sydney

No part of this publication may be reproduced in whole or in part, or stored in a retrieval system, or transmitted in any form or by any means, electronic, mechanical, photocopying, recording, or otherwise, without written permission of the publisher. For information regarding permission, write to Scholastic Inc., 555 Broadway, New York, NY 10012.

ISBN 0-590-22852-8

Copyright © 1995 by Todd Strasser.
All rights reserved. Published by Scholastic Inc.
APPLE PAPERBACKS® is a registered trademark of Scholastic Inc.

12 11 10 9 8 7 6 5 4 3 2 1   5 6 7 8 9/9 0/0

Printed in the U.S.A.   40

First Scholastic printing, January 1995

To Ken and Gladys

ABE LINCOLN FOR CLASS PRESIDENT!

1

It was our first day back at school after Christmas vacation, and no one was happy about it. The only thing I was happy about was that it was finally snowing. Outside white snowflakes were drifting slowly down and covering the frozen gray-and-brown earth. That meant that I'd finally be able to use the snowblower I'd bought over the summer to make money clearing driveways.

I took my seat in homeroom near Ricky Detrich. Ricky was a short brown-haired kid with big ears who played guard with me on the Putney basketball team.

"Maybe they'll close school early today," he said.

"They never close school early," said his twin sister Sabrina, who was blond and had small ears. Ricky and Sabrina were twins, but not identical. They were always fighting with each other.

"Sure, they do," Ricky said, turning to me. "Don't they, Max?"

I shrugged. The last thing I wanted to do was get in the middle of a Ricky-Sabrina fight.

The other kids came in, including my neighbor and closest friend, Cody Barnes. Cody was the tallest girl in school. Actually, after Dave Short, she was the second tallest *person* in school. She had long brown hair that she always wore in a braid. She also had freckles and brown eyes. Cody had gone away skiing over Christmas and this was the first time I'd seen her since she got back.

"Hi, Max." She smiled at me and sat down. "How was vacation?"

"Okay," I said. "How was skiing?"

"Great," she said. She had a strange, dreamy look on her face that I'd never seen before. "Only, I missed you."

"Oh?" I didn't know what to say. Cody had never said anything like that to me before. "Well, here I am."

It looked like Cody was going to say something more, but then Ms. Schmidt entered the room. She was a thin lady with short black hair and big colorful earrings. She was our homeroom teacher, and we also took English and social studies with her. Sometimes it was hard to remember which was which, especially after a long vacation. But I was pretty sure this was social studies.

"As you may recall, we were studying American history before Christmas break," she said, taking some papers out of her desk. "Does anyone have any questions before we continue?"

"Yeah." Ricky raised his hand. "When's our *next* vacation?"

"You get Martin Luther King's birthday off on January 17," Ms. Schmidt said. "And then you get Presidents' Day off in February. That reminds me, what shall we do for Presidents' Day this year?"

"Stay home!" Ricky yelled.

"I'm not related to him," his sister Sabrina muttered, rolling her eyes.

"I know," Ms. Schmidt said. "Why don't we do a — "

"Don't say it, Ms. Schmidt!" groaned Dave Short. He had red hair and the worst case of zits in the whole grade. He played center for the Putney basketball team.

"Yeah, not *another* play," said Ricky.

"Why not?" Ms. Schmidt asked.

"Because that's all we *ever* do," Dave said.

"Would you rather do reports?" Ms. Schmidt asked.

Everyone in the class looked around at one other. There were eighteen of us, and we were the entire eighth grade at the Putney K-8 School.

"On second thought, maybe a play would be fun," Ricky said.

"Yeah, we haven't done one in at least three weeks," added Dave.

3

"So what will this one be about?" Ms. Schmidt asked.

"I know!" Brian Dent waved his hand excitedly. Brian had neatly parted brown hair. He wore a clean red and green plaid shirt and pressed khaki pants. He had to pass his mother's inspection each morning before he went to school.

"We'll do a play about this class and all they ever do is plays," Brian said. "And after a while they can't tell what's real and what's a play anymore. And then they get kidnapped by aliens. And it turns out these aliens live on a planet where everyone's an actor. And they need new plays to perform. And there's this evil emperor — "

"That sounds very interesting, Brian," Ms. Schmidt said patiently. "But keep in mind this is a play about Presidents' Day."

"Well, yeah," Brian said. "There could be presidents, too. See, it turns out that these aliens have a time machine and they've gone into the past and kidnapped all the presidents because they figured they'd have good material for more plays — "

Brian lived next to Cody. The three of us had grown up together. Cody and I had gotten into sports and Brian had just gotten weird. Then again, if Cody or I had Brian's mother, we probably would have gotten weird, too.

All at once the long white fluorescent lights above us flickered, then flashed brightly.

4

Pop! Bzzzzzzz . . . a fluorescent bulb overhead burned out and the room dimmed slightly.

"There goes another one," said Ricky.

Ms. Schmidt stared up at the ceiling and shook her head. "I wish they'd figure out what's wrong already."

For the past week, lights all over the town of Putney had been going dim, flickering, getting too bright, and blowing out.

"Do they know what the problem is yet?" Cody asked.

"They know it's somewhere in the relay station from the power plant," Ms. Schmidt said. "But they can't figure out why we get these surges and brownouts."

Sabrina raised her hand. She had pale skin and no freckles.

"Yes, Sabrina?" Ms. Schmidt called on her.

"Presidents' Day is about Lincoln and Washington, so why don't we do a play where one of them comes from the past and into the present?" she said. "He could actually come to this school. The plot would be about how we have to get him back to the past, but in the meantime we could learn all about him."

Sabrina was always coming up with ideas like that. Sometimes we called her Sa*brain*a.

Ms. Schmidt looked surprised. "Why, that's an excellent idea."

"Excuse me, Ms. Schmidt?" Brian raised his hand.

"Yes, Brian?"

"That really wouldn't work."

Ms. Schmidt's forehead wrinkled. "Why not?"

"The space-time continuum won't allow anyone from the past to have a memory of it when they come into the present," Brian said. "It would violate the historical paradox."

"*You're* the historical paradox," Ricky snickered.

Brian narrowed his eyes at Ricky.

Ms. Schmidt looked uncertain. I knew what she was probably thinking. Where did Brian come up with this stuff?

"Well, you're probably right, Brian," she said. "But this is only a play."

"Are we gonna have to wear costumes?" Dave asked with a pained look.

"I'm sure we'll find everything we need in the costume closet," Ms. Schmidt replied, pointing at the large closet in the back of the room where she kept a collection of costumes.

Cody raised her hand. "What will George Washington or Abe Lincoln do while they're here?"

"I know!" Brian waved his hand again. "He could be the president who got away from the aliens! He could talk about how he escaped."

"Mega psychobunny," Ricky whispered.

"That's enough, Ricky." Ms. Schmidt shot him a look and and then spoke patiently to Brian. "In order for this to be an educational project, I think it should be based on historical facts."

Now Dave raised his hand.

"Yes, Dave?"

"Why do we have to do something about Presidents' Day anyway?"

"Because Presidents Washington and Lincoln were extremely important men," Ms. Schmidt said. "Some people think they were the two most influential figures in our nation's history."

"But that was a long time ago," Dave said. "I mean, they've been dead, like, forever."

"But they're part of history," Ms. Schmidt said.

"So?" Ricky said. "Why do we have to learn about all that stuff? It's got nothing to do with our lives today."

"It's got *everything* to do with our lives today," Ms. Schmidt replied. "If it hadn't been for Washington and Lincoln, our lives today might be completely different."

The bell was about to ring and kids started to pull out their backpacks.

"So which president should we focus on?" Ms. Schmidt asked.

"Which is the guy on the penny?" Ricky asked.

"Lincoln, you nitwit," Sabrina groaned.

"Yes, let's do Lincoln," Ms. Schmidt said. "So

your assignment tonight will be to read about Lincoln and come up with one question you would ask him if you met him today."

Briinnnggg! The bell rang and we started to get out of our seats. Once again, I noticed that Cody was giving me that funny, dreamy look.

"Didn't you miss me?" she asked.

"Gee, Cody, you were only gone for two weeks," I said.

Cody looked disappointed. Something weird was going on.

2

Our next class was gym. Since we were such a small grade and had a lot of the same classes, we usually walked around school in a group.

"Not another play," Dave said, shaking his head as we walked down the hall.

"Ms. Schmidt's just a frustrated actress," Sabrina said.

"It beats having to write a report," added Ricky.

"I just have this really bad feeling she's gonna pick me to be Lincoln," Dave said. "I've managed to get out of every play since the third grade. I just *know* she's gonna nail me this time."

"He *was* very tall," Sabrina said.

"If it's just one president, what are the rest of us gonna do?" I asked.

"We could be the aliens," said Brian.

"Will you chill with those aliens already?" Ricky

snapped. "And what was that junk about a power box?"

"Not a power box, a paradox," Brian said. "It's just that people can't move around in time taking their knowledge with them. It would mess everything up."

"When did *you* become such an expert in time travel?" Ricky asked.

"I've, uh, been doing research," Brian said.

"History is so boring," I said. "Why can't we study something that really affects us?"

"Like what?" Cody asked.

"Like why we have to go to school," Ricky said.

We got to the gym and left our backpacks in the hallway. The gym, like everything else at Putney, was small and old. It even *smelled* old. Inside, the boys and girls separated. The girls went into the gymnastics room while the boys stayed in the gym for basketball.

Cody was the one exception. The year before, she had received special permission from the state to join the Putney School basketball team. She was the only girl in the league, and probably one of its best forwards. So when the boys had basketball in gym, she played with us.

I got changed quickly and went out into the gym to take some warm-up shots. Cody joined me.

"I think the Presidents' Day project sounds interesting," she said as she shot from the foul line.

"You do?" I gave her a surprised look.

"Only because we can trace my mother's family almost all the way back to the pilgrims," she said. "Actually, my great-great-great-grandmother was a nurse in a hospital during the Civil War. She took care of my great-great-great-grand-father, who was a Union soldier."

"I didn't know that," I said.

Cody nodded. "So that part of history is sort of interesting to me. Like, how it affected my family."

"Well, one of them became the first girl bas-ketball player ever to play on the Putney team," I said. "That's pretty historic."

I expected Cody to grin, but she just shrugged.

"What's wrong?" I asked.

Before Cody could answer, the rest of the kids came out of the locker room and joined us. A mo-ment later Mr. Neal Anderthal, otherwise known as Coach Neanderthal, came in.

Coach Neanderthal taught shop, gym, and coached basketball. He was a stocky man with a low forehead and deep-set eyes. He was the hair-iest person I'd ever seen. Thick dark hair grew out of his nose and his ears. The backs of his hands looked like paws. He always wore a blue warm-up suit and walked around with a basketball under his arm.

Soooooweeeeeeet! Coach Neanderthal stuck his thumb and index finger into his mouth and whis-tled. He was very proud that he didn't need a metal referee's whistle like most coaches. He could just stick his fingers in his mouth and blow.

"All right, boys, choose up sides!" he shouted. His voice echoed through the little gym.

"Ahem!" Cody cleared her throat.

"Er, boys and girl," Coach Neanderthal corrected himself.

We played for about twenty minutes and then Neanderthal stuck his fingers in his mouth and whistled again. "Okay, boys, take a break."

"Ahem." Cody wiped some sweat off her forehead.

"Uh, I meant, boys *and girl*," Neanderthal said. "Cody and Max, front and center."

The other kids went to the water fountain while Cody and I walked over to the coach. Cody and I were co-captains of the Putney basketball team.

"You know I'm retiring after this year," Coach Neanderthal said.

Cody and I were both surprised. Neanderthal had been our gym teacher since kindergarten. It was hard to imagine Putney School without him standing in the gym in his blue warm-up suit with a basketball under his arm.

"I've put in my twenty-five years," he said. "Now it's time to relax. There's just one thing I regret. In all the years I've coached this team, my boys have never had a winning season."

"Ahem." Cody cleared her throat.

"Uh, my players, that is," Neanderthal said.

We'd already played three games that season. Our record was one win and two losses.

"It's not easy when the whole seventh and eighth grade combined is less than fifty kids," I said. "I mean, we play schools where there are *two hundred* kids per grade."

"Oh, I know there are plenty of good reasons for losing," Neanderthal said. "But still, all I ever wanted was that one winning season."

"There's still this year," Cody said.

Behind us, Ricky and Dave went back on the gym floor and practiced dribbling the ball down the court. Ricky bounce-passed it to Dave. No one was defending the basket, and it should have been an easy layup, but Dave bobbled the ball and it bounced out of bounds. Neanderthal winced.

"Come on, Short, concentrate!" he shouted. Then he turned back to us. "Not with 'Stone Hands' Short at center," he said under his breath. "It'll take a miracle for us to have a winning season *this* year."

I glanced at Cody, and knew what she was thinking. We both felt bad that Coach Neanderthal was going to retire without ever having a winning team. But, hey, it wasn't the end of the world.

3

Most afternoons, Cody, Brian, and I walked home together. Like I said, Brian was Cody's other next door neighbor, which meant he lived two doors down from me.

We waited by the school's front door for Brian, who was late as usual. Snow had been falling all day and now the ground was covered with about four inches of the white stuff.

"Looks like snowblower time," I said with a smile.

"Now?" Cody asked.

"Better believe it," I said. "I'll do my driveway first. Then yours. Then Mr. Paterson's. It'll be a piece of cake now that I have the snowblower. And tomorrow after school I'll do the Bergers' driveway, and the Cushings' and the Browns'."

Cody raised her eyebrows. "You've made deals to do *all* those driveways this winter?"

"Every time it snows," I said proudly.

Cody smiled weakly and gazed outside. I could tell something was bothering her.

"What's wrong?" I asked.

Cody looked back at me, surprised. "Who said anything was wrong?"

"You've been acting weird all day," I said. "Did something happen over vacation?"

Cody studied me for a moment with her clear brown eyes. Then she said, "Max, I want to ask you something because you're my closest and oldest friend, but you have to promise not to laugh, okay?"

"Uh, okay." This was strange. Cody *never* talked to me like this.

She took a deep breath and let it out slowly. "Max, do you think I'm pretty?"

"Gee, Cody, I, er, don't know what to say. I've never really thought about it."

Cody nodded sadly, as if I'd confirmed some fear she had.

"I mean, I'm not saying you're not," I said.

"That's what happened over vacation," Cody said. "I saw all these girls my age at the hotel. They were pretty, and they wore nice clothes and did nice things with their hair. And I realized I was just this girl basketball player. I mean, sometimes I think that because I'm tall, everyone, including me, forgets that I'm also a girl."

I really didn't know what to say. In a way she

15

was right. Cody and I had been friends and teammates for so long that I really didn't think of her . . . as a girl.

"Hey, guys, sorry I'm late." Brian jogged up to us, pulling on his jacket. "Mr. Wells and I got into a discussion about quantum mechanics and I forgot the time."

"Quantum mechanics?" I scowled.

"It's just a mathematical theory dealing with the interactions of matter and radiation." Brian explained, like it was no big deal. "It has some interesting implications in terms of time travel."

Cody and I glanced at each other and rolled our eyes. Then we pushed through the front door and went out into the cold. The snow was light and powdery and easy to walk through.

"Great," I said. "This looks like a lot of snow, but the snowblower will cut through it in no time. I might even be able to get the Bergers' driveway done tonight."

"What about homework?" Cody asked as we walked.

"I'll do it in school tomorrow," I said.

"Did you get any books?" she asked.

"About what?" I asked.

Cody gave me a look. "Lincoln. Remember Ms. Schmidt said she wanted ideas for the play tomorrow?"

"Oh, right." I'd forgotten. "Okay, first thing in the morning I'll go to the library."

"Too late," Cody said. "You know how small the library is. All the books on Lincoln were taken out by lunchtime."

"Did you get any?" I asked.

Cody shook her head. White clumps of snow stuck to her brown hair. "Sabrina let me look at her books during study hall so I did it then."

"What about you?" I asked Brian.

"I'll just go on the Net," Brian said.

"The Net?"

"Internet," Brian said. "The worldwide database of computers. You can use it too if you want, Max."

"Thanks," I said, "but won't we both get the same information?"

"Don't worry," Brian said. "There'll be plenty for both of us. After all, it's the information superhighway."

"Okay, Brian, I will."

We got to Brian's house and said good-bye to Cody, who continued on to her house next door. Brian and I trudged up his front path through the snow. Like everything else in Putney, Brian's house was old, with wooden shutters on the windows and whitish smoke curling out of the chimney.

But inside, Brian's house was different from most other houses. It was spotless.

"You know we have to leave our shoes here," Brian said, just inside the front door. "And you have to wash your hands."

17

"My hands are pretty clean," I said.

"Doesn't matter," Brian said. "You know the rules."

Brian's house had a million rules. You couldn't wear shoes inside. You had to wash your hands, and you weren't allowed to touch the walls. All the floors were covered with clear plastic runners. Brian used to have a father, but he broke too many rules and had to move out. Now Mr. Dent lived in the next town over.

I went into the powder room and washed my hands. When I came out, Mrs. Dent was standing in the hall with Brian. She was a small thin woman with wrinkled skin. She always squinted as if she were on a constant lookout for dirt.

"You didn't tell me you were bringing a friend home," she said to Brian.

"It was a last-minute thing, Mom," Brian tried to explain.

"You know the rules," Mrs. Dent said. "You have to give me forty-eight hours notice before you bring anyone into this house."

"Hi, Mrs. Dent." I gave her a little wave.

Mrs. Dent squinted at me. "Hello, Max. Is anyone at your house sick?"

"No."

"Good, I wouldn't want you carrying any diseases into our home."

"Wouldn't think of it, Mrs. Dent," I said.

"Mom, I invited Max over because he needs to

get some information on my computer," Brian explained. "It's the only way he'll get his homework done."

"You couldn't give him the information over the phone?" Mrs. Dent asked.

"Well, then it would be like me doing his homework for him," Brian said.

"Hmmm." Mrs. Dent turned to me. "Let me see your hands, Max."

I showed her my hands.

"All right, I'll make an exception just this once," Mrs. Dent said. "You can go into Brian's room only, Max. And please stay on the plastic runners and try not to touch the walls."

"Right, Mrs. Dent," I said.

Brian and I started down the hall.

"Brian, where are you going?" she asked. "Your after-school snack is waiting in the kitchen."

"I'm not really hungry, Mom," Brian said.

Mrs. Dent put her hands on her hips and squinted at him. "You know the rules, Brian. You must have milk and cookies every day after school."

"Okay." Brian nodded with a sigh. "I'll get to it in a second. I just want to show Max how to use the computer."

We followed the plastic runner down to Brian's room.

"I haven't seen your mom in a long time," I said as Brian closed the bedroom door behind us.

"She's so busy cleaning, she never has time to leave the house," he said.

I could see what he meant. Brian's room was spotless and perfectly organized. On his desk was a super-clean computer.

"You know how to use a computer, right?" he asked.

"Pretty much," I said.

"I'll put you into the Harvard University historical reference area," Brian said, sitting down at the desk. "The only thing I'm worried about are those power surges. My old surge protector broke and I haven't gotten a new one yet."

"What'll happen if we get a power surge while I'm using the computer?" I asked.

"It could really mess up my time machine," Brian said.

4

I stared at him like he was crazy. "Time machine?"

"See all these cables?" Brian asked. He pointed at a thick bundle of tightly wrapped cables that went out the back of the computer, along the baseboard on the wall, and into his closet.

"Yeah?"

Brian got up and opened his closet. Inside, it looked like a normal closet except that the walls, floor, and ceiling were covered with shiny metal foil.

"I told my mom the foil helps keep insects out," Brian said, "but actually it's a time machine."

"Your closet?" I asked.

"Yup."

"Why did you turn your closet into a time machine?" I asked, still not quite believing him.

"It's just the right size."

"Yeah, but why build a time machine?"

"Are you kidding?" Brian asked. "If you had my mother, wouldn't *you* want to get away?"

"Well, have you gone anywhere yet?" I asked.

"No, I'm still running unmanneds," Brian said. "The other day I sent my hamster back to the Dark Ages."

"What happened?"

"He didn't come back," Brian said with a shrug. "Maybe he liked it better."

I looked at him in disbelief. "Brian, have you told anyone about this?"

"Forget about telling anyone," he said. "I just want to make sure it works and then get out of here. If she makes me wash my hands one more time, I'm going to become a serial killer or something."

"But don't you think . . ." I started to say.

Brian gave me a serious look. "Listen, Max, you and I have known each other since we were two years old. I know in recent years we haven't been that friendly because you became a jock and I became a brainiac, but I still consider you one of my closest friends. That's why I'm going to ask you to swear, on all the years we've known each other, that you won't tell anyone about this until after I'm gone."

"But — "

"Once I'm gone, you have to destroy this machine," Brian said.

"Why?" I asked, dumbfounded.

"Because if you don't, she'll come after me," Brian said. "That's why I can't just run away. Wherever I went, she'd find me. My only chance is to get into another time dimension completely."

I was speechless.

"So swear you won't tell anyone," Brian said.

"I . . . I . . . what about Cody?"

Brian thought for a moment. "Okay, you can tell Cody, but you have to make her swear she won't tell anyone."

"I swear," I said.

"Good." Brian closed the closet door and sat down at the computer again. "Now let's look up Lincoln."

It didn't take long for Brian to get all sorts of information about Lincoln on the computer screen.

"Okay," he said, "here's what you need. I have to go have my after-school snack. I'll be back later."

Brian left and I started to take notes. It turned out that Lincoln grew up really poor and his father was anti-slavery. I was just starting to read about his life as a teenager when the lights in Brian's room suddenly dimmed and flickered.

It must have been another power surge!

Remembering what Brian had said about a power surge messing up his time machine, I quickly looked for something that would turn off the computer. Next to the computer was a row of switches including a big red one. Red usually meant off, so I quickly flicked it.

Phooooom! There was a flash of light inside Brian's closet and strange-looking vapors started to seep out around the door. I stared back at the red switch.

Oh, no! In tiny, neat letters it said TIME MACHINE.

I'd hit the wrong button!

"Max?" It was Brian, calling from downstairs. "The computer okay?"

"Uh, sure, yeah. Everything's fine, just fine," I shouted back, not wanting him to come up and discover that I might have just destroyed his time machine. I quickly picked up my notebook and left the room. As I went downstairs and passed the kitchen, I waved at Brian, who was sitting at the kitchen table, having chocolate chip cookies and milk.

"Going already?" He looked surprised.

"Uh, yeah."

"Did you get the information you needed?" he asked.

"I think so."

Little did I know. . . .

5

I lived two houses down from Brian's. My house was dark and empty as usual. My parents were both accountants, and this was the beginning of tax season. I wouldn't see much of them from now until April 15.

But I was used to that, and besides, I had my snow removal business to attend to. So I went out to the garage, got the snowblower, and went to work.

When I got back home around seven o'clock, I'd actually managed to get all the driveways done. The snow was so light and fluffy that the snowblower went through it in no time. I came back into the house. Mom and Dad were sitting at the kitchen table with their glasses on. They were reading through piles of papers while they ate Chinese food from white take-out containers.

"He wants to deduct a percentage of the second car as a business expense," my father was saying. He was bald and chubby and wore thick glasses.

"How does he justify it?" asked my mother. She was chubby and also wore thick glasses. But she wasn't bald.

"He drives it when the first car is in the shop," my father said.

"Twenty-five percent," said my mother.

"Hi, guys," I said.

"Hi, Max," my father said and turned back to my mother. "He wants to take fifty percent. He says the car's in the shop a lot."

"Hi, Max," said my mother, who then turned to my father. "You won't get away with more than thirty-five, I promise."

"Uh, any phone calls?" I asked.

"Brian," said my mother.

Uh-oh. I was afraid of that. He must have discovered that I messed up his time machine. I went upstairs and called on the phone in my parents' bedroom.

"Hello?" It was Mrs. Dent.

"Uh, hi, it's Max. Brian there?"

"Just a minute."

"Hello?" Brian got on.

"Hi, it's Max."

"Mom?" Brian said. "You still on the phone?"

His mother didn't answer.

"Mom, I didn't hear the phone click, so I know you're still listening," Brian said. "Mom, please get off the phone."

"You know the rule, Brian," his mother said. "No phone calls after nine o'clock."

"Mom, it's five minutes after seven," Brian said.

"I'm just reminding you." *Click!* She hung up.

For a moment there was silence.

"Hear any breathing?" Brian asked.

"No."

"Good. Sometimes she doesn't really get off the phone. But then I hear her breathing."

"So what's up?" I asked.

"You have to come over right now," Brian said.

"Why?" I asked.

"I can't tell you over the phone," Brian said. "And you can't come in the front door because I'm not allowed to have friends over after dinner. Just come around to my window. I'll let out the emergency fire ladder."

"What's this about?" I asked.

"Just get over here," Brian said. "Fast."

I went back downstairs. Mom and Dad were still huddled over their papers.

"They want to apply last year's expenses to this year's deductions," Dad was saying.

"I'm going out," I said. "See you later."

"Bye." Mom waved and turned back to Dad. "What kind of documentation do they have?"

Outside I cut through Cody's snowy, dark backyard and into Brian's backyard. Brian was just letting a metal rope ladder down from his window.

"It's secure," he whispered.

I grabbed the ladder and climbed up. Brian helped me through the window and into the room. He'd laid out newspaper on the floor. "Take off your shoes."

"Okay, but what's going on?" I asked. I sat down on the corner of his bed to pull off my shoes.

"This." Brian walked to his closet and opened it. Inside was a tall thin guy with coarse black hair that sort of stuck out in strange ways. He had thick eyebrows, high cheekbones, and a gaunt look. His shirt was patched and his pants looked like they'd been sewn by hand. He was barefoot and holding a pair of old-fashioned brown leather boots under his arm.

He looked exactly like a young Abe Lincoln.

6

"No!" I gasped. The shoe I had just taken off fell out of my hands to the floor.

"Yes." Brian closed the closet door. "Something happened before, didn't it?"

I knew I had to tell him the truth. "It was an accident. I was trying to turn the computer off so it wouldn't be damaged by the power surge. I accidentally hit the time machine switch instead."

Brian nodded. "I figured."

I pointed at the closet. "Is that really *him?*"

"Yes."

"Can't you send him back?"

"Not right away," Brian said. "First I have to do some research and find out where he was at that age. We can't send him back to Illinois if he was in Indiana. It could totally mess up history."

"Can't you just *ask* him?"

Brian opened the closet door again. Young Abe was still standing there. It was sort of odd that he hadn't moved.

"What's your name?" Brian asked.

Young Abe frowned. "I don't know."

"Where're you from?" Brian asked.

"I don't know."

Brian closed the door again and turned back to me. "See? It's the space-time continuum. He doesn't remember anything."

"I bet he's wondering why he's in your closet," I said.

Brian opened the closet door. Abe looked at us.

"Are you wondering why you're in this closet?" Brian asked.

Abe nodded.

Brian closed the closet door again and turned to me. "Well, I've got news for you, he's not going to wonder for long because he's not going to be in there for long."

"Why not?"

"Because you're going to take him home while I figure out where he's going back in time," Brian said.

"Why can't he stay here?" I asked.

"Are you serious?" Brian asked. "What do you think'll happen if my mother finds him?"

"Don't tell her," I said. "Can't you hide him in the closet?"

"No way," said Brian. "She cleans the closet every morning at exactly eleven-oh-seven."

"Well, what am I going to do with him?" I asked.

"I don't know," Brian said. "All I know is you better not let anything bad happen to him. He was one of the most important men in our country's history. If he doesn't get back to where he's supposed to be, things are going to get really messed up."

"What if I don't want him?" I asked.

"Hey, listen," Brian said. "If it wasn't for me you'd be going to school tomorrow without your homework. You *owe* me."

"All I wanted was some *information* about the guy," I said. "I didn't want the guy *himself*."

"Tough," Brian said.

Great. Now I was stuck with Abe Lincoln. The whole history of our country rested on my shoulders. I stood up.

"You have to take the other shoe off," Brian said.

"Give it a rest."

"I'm serious," he said. "My mom'll see the footprint."

I took off the other shoe. Then I walked over to the closet, and opened the door. Young Abe looked down at me.

"Wow, he's tall," I said.

"For his time he was extremely tall," Brian said. "Possibly the tallest person most people had ever seen."

"So listen," I said to Abe. "I guess you're coming to my house tonight."

Abe nodded. "Can I put my boots back on? My feet are cold."

I looked down at his feet. Abe had the biggest feet I'd ever seen. And they were ugly, too. I turned to Brian. "Gee, did you see this guy's feet?"

Abe and Brian both looked down. Abe's feet were gnarly and calloused and his toenails were long and dirty. Some curled. Others were split and broken.

"What's wrong with them?" Abe asked.

"You have to remember, Max," Brian said. "He probably goes barefoot around the woods all summer."

"Well, he really ought to get a pedicure while he's here," I said.

"Listen, Abe, you can't put your boots back on until you get over here on the newspaper," Brian said.

Abe went over to the newspaper. He and I put our shoes on. Then we helped Abe out the window and he climbed down. I started to go out the window next, but halfway out I stopped and looked back at Brian.

"What does he eat?" I asked.

"Stick with meat and potatoes," Brian said.

"All we have is leftover Chinese."

Brian rolled his eyes. "Good luck."

I climbed down the ladder and joined Abe in the snow.

"It's not far," I said. We started to cut through Cody's backyard. Abe kept looking around.

"Does everyone live in these?" he asked.

"Yeah, they're called houses," I said.

We got back to my house and went in the front door. Mom and Dad were still in the kitchen with their tax papers.

"She says that's all she made," my father was saying.

"Did you ask her how she can afford that condo in Florida?" replied my mother.

"Uh, excuse me," I said. Abe and I stood in the kitchen doorway. Mom and Dad looked up.

"This is, uh, Abe," I said.

"Hi, Abe," my mother said. My father didn't look up. He was busy crunching numbers on his calculator.

"Abe's going to be staying with us for a while," I said.

"The carrying costs on the condo alone are fifteen thou," my father said.

"That's nice, dear," said my mom. "And if you add the house in Scarsdale, she *has* to be making more."

"Uh, is there anything to eat?" I asked.

"Check the fridge," Mom said.

"We're simply going to have to tell her that we know she isn't declaring all her income," Dad said.

I checked in the refrigerator. It was mostly old

Chinese takeout containers. "Uh, I think I'm gonna order in a pizza."

"Fine," Mom said. "Don't these people realize that we have to be responsible about these things?"

I took Abe up to my room. He stood there, looking around at my basketball posters and stuff.

"You can sit on the bed," I said.

Abe sat down and put his hands on his knees.

"Don't you know who you are?" I asked.

"I'm Abe," he said.

"Do you know where you're from?"

Abe shook his head.

Whew, I thought, what am I gonna do with this guy? "Don't you remember *anything*?" I asked.

"I was over there." He pointed toward Brian's house.

Great. I was stuck with this guy and he didn't know a thing. Then I had an idea. "Wait here for a second," I said. I went into my parents' bedroom and dialed Cody's number.

"Hello?"

"Cody, it's Max."

"Oh, hi."

"Could you come over here for a second?"

"Now? Why?"

"I have someone I'd like you to meet."

"Who?"

"Just come over."

34

"But it's cold and snowy out."

"It's important," I said and hung up.

I went back into my bedroom. Abe was still sitting on the bed.

"So, uh, what do you like to do?" I asked.

Abe shrugged.

"Are you hungry?" I asked.

Abe nodded. Then I realized he'd just taken a really long trip.

"Need to use the bathroom?"

Abe scowled. It occurred to me that he didn't know what a bathroom was.

"Come with me," I said.

We went down the hall to the bathroom. Abe looked around and frowned. I pointed at the toilet.

"See, this is where you, uh . . . you. . . ." How was I going to explain this? "Look, Abe, you're a smart guy. You get the idea, right? And you can do this." I flushed the toilet.

When the toilet flushed, Abe jumped about three feet with surprise. Then he bent forward and stared into the toilet bowl.

"I'll just wait out here, okay?" I said.

I left him in the bathroom and closed the door. Then I put my ear to the door and listened to make sure Abe understood what I'd said.

"What are you doing?"

I spun around and found Cody climbing the stairs. I felt my face turn red.

"Gee, you got here quick."

"What's going on in the bathroom?" Cody asked.

"Uh, I was just trying to make sure he knew what to do."

Cody gave me a funny look. "Who?"

"Cody, you're not gonna believe this."

"Try me."

"Abraham Lincoln's in my bathroom."

7

Cody smiled. "Very funny."

"I'm serious," I said. "You *have* to believe me."

Cody looked at the bathroom door and then back at me. "I'm supposed to believe that the sixteenth president of the United States, a man who's been dead for more than a hundred years, is in your bathroom?"

"Uh-huh."

"Do your parents know about this?" Cody asked.

"Sort of."

Inside the bathroom, the toilet flushed.

"Hey, Abe," I said, turning toward the door. "You can wash your hands if you like. You turn those silver knobs over the sink and water comes out."

I heard the faucet start to run. One thing you could say about Abe, he learned fast.

Cody stared at me for a second. "Max, I think we better go talk to your parents."

Inside the bathroom, the water stopped. The bathroom door swung open. Cody's and Abe's eyes met.

Cody turned and glared at me. "Give me a break, Max, that's not . . ." She stopped and looked back at Abe again.

"Gee, you're tall," she said.

"He was possibly the tallest person most people had ever seen back in the 1800s," I said.

Cody looked at Abe's face, then at his patched shirt, homemade pants, and old-fashioned boots.

"Ahhhh!" she gasped.

It took a while for Cody to recover from her shock. By then the pizza had come. We sat on my bedroom floor eating and drinking soda. Abe picked up a piece of pizza and started to eat it crust first.

"No, look, here's the best way," I said, folding my pizza in half lengthwise and starting from the pointy end.

Abe quickly got the idea.

"Could you explain how this happened?" Cody said.

I explained about Brian's time machine and made Cody swear she wouldn't tell anyone.

"I don't belong here?" Abe asked.

"No, man, you belong back in the 1800s," I said.

"You're going to become one of the country's greatest presidents," Cody said.

"What's a president?"

"It's like you get to tell everyone what to do," I said.

"You're going to free the slaves," Cody said.

Abe took a gulp of Coke. "What's a slave?"

"How come he doesn't know anything?" Cody asked.

"It's got something to do with the space-time continuum," I said. "Remember Brian said something about the historical paradox?"

"Why didn't Brian send him right back?" Cody asked.

I explained how Brian had to research exactly where Abe had come from so we didn't send him back to the wrong place.

"Well, shouldn't we tell someone?" Cody asked.

"No way," I said. "Just think of what could happen if people found out. The government would probably take him away, and then history would get completely messed up. Or maybe he'd get kidnapped by spies or something. Besides, if people find out about Brian's time machine, he'll probably never be able to escape his mother."

I turned to Abe. "Listen, you can't tell anyone who you really are, okay? It's really important."

"You don't think your parents are going to suspect something strange?" Cody asked. "I mean, he *looks* just like Abe Lincoln and we call him Abe."

"You're right," I said. "We're gonna have to come up with a new name for him."

Abe was looking at my posters of basketball players again. Then I remembered something I'd read about him that afternoon.

"Hey, didn't Lincoln come from Indiana?" I asked.

"They moved there from Kentucky," said Cody.

"Well, Larry Bird was from Indiana," I said, referring to the great Celtics star from the 1980s. "Let's call him Larry."

"Larry Lincoln?" Cody made a face. "Sounds like a dork."

"Hey, come on," I said. "He's not gonna be here that long. It doesn't matter." I turned to Abe. "From now on, your name is Larry Lincoln, okay?"

Abe, I mean, Larry, nodded.

"So what are you going to do with him?" Cody asked.

"I guess I'll just keep him here."

"Won't your parents mind?"

"Mind? I doubt they'll even notice," I said.

"May I?" Abe, I mean, Larry, had finished his slice and was pointing at another one.

"Dig in," I said.

Larry picked up another slice, folded it like a pro, and took a bite.

"Don't you remember *anything?*" Cody asked him.

"I was in a little room surrounded by silver," Larry said, while he chewed on a mouthful of pizza.

"Brian's closet, where the time machine is," I explained.

"Then I was in a room where I couldn't wear my shoes," said Larry.

"Brian's bedroom," I explained.

"Then we climbed down a ladder, went through the snow, and came here." Larry swallowed and held out his cup. "May I have more?"

"Sure." I filled his cup with soda.

Larry took a gulp and smiled. "Thank you for this fine meal."

"No sweat," I said.

Cody just stared at him. "I really, *really* don't believe this."

Larry slept in a sleeping bag on the floor. He stayed in my room all week while I went to school. On Thursday afternoon, the basketball team lost to Brunswick, making our record one win and three losses. We really should have won the game, but Dave dropped an easy pass in the final seconds and the other team got the ball and scored. Coach

Neanderthal screamed at him the whole game. Afterwards Dave said the reason he'd dropped the ball was because he couldn't concentrate. All he could think about was how he was probably going to have to be Lincoln in Ms. Schmidt's play.

Friday afternoon after school, Brian, Cody, and I walked home together.

"How much longer until you send him back, Brian?" I asked.

"Not much," Brian said. "I've sent E-mail to every historian on the Internet, asking for information about exactly where Lincoln was living when he was in his early teens. I should have the answer any day now."

"What's he been doing all week?" Cody asked.

"Not much," I said. "He just sits in my room and reads."

"He must be totally bored," she said.

"I know," I said. "I came home last night and he was reading my fifth-grade math book. I'm really starting to feel sorry for the guy."

"Maybe we should take him out tonight," Cody said. "Like to the mall or something."

"Are you serious?" I asked.

"Why not?" Cody said. "If anyone asks, we'll just tell them he's your cousin, visiting from out of town."

"But his clothes . . ." I said.

"He looks like he's the same size as Brett," Cody said. Brett was her older brother, who went to high school. "I can borrow some of his clothes."

I gave Brian a questioning look.

"I guess it's okay," Brian said. "Just make sure nothing happens to him."

"Maybe you should come with us," I said.

"And miss Star Trek?" Brian looked at us like we were crazy. "Besides, I hate hanging around the mall."

Cody turned to me. "I'll pick out some of Brett's clothes and come by in an hour."

"Sure."

Brian and Cody said good-bye at their houses and I continued to mine. I let myself in, but as I went past the kitchen, I noticed my mom was in there working at the kitchen table. She must've come home early from work.

"Max?" she said, tipping her eye-glasses down.

"Oh, hi, Mom, home early, huh?"

"Could you come in here, please?" she said. I could tell by the tone of her voice that something was wrong.

"Uh, sure," I said nervously. "What's up?"

"There's a young man in your room," she said. "I'd like to know who he is."

8

Young man?" I swallowed.

"Yes," Mom said. "He's tall and has black hair. I asked him who he was and where he lived. He said his name was Larry and he lived here."

"Oh, yeah, well, remember I brought him home a couple of days ago?" I said. Hoping she wouldn't remember that I'd introduced him as Abe.

"You didn't tell us he was going to live here," Mom said.

"Well, er . . ." I didn't know what to say. Cody and I had just agreed that we'd tell people Larry, I mean, Abe, was my cousin. But I couldn't tell my mother that because she *knew* all my cousins.

"Uh, don't you remember I told you about that foreign exchange student?" I said.

Mom frowned. "No."

"Oh, yeah," I said. "He was supposed to stay with my friend Jake from school. But Jake's brother has the measles so I said he could stay with us."

"Shouldn't you have asked us first?" Mom said.

"I did," I said.

"When?"

"Uh, one night when you and Dad were working on tax stuff."

Mom shook her head. "I can't remember, but if you say you did, I believe you. How long will he stay with us?"

"Just until Jake's brother gets over the measles," I said.

"All right." Mom nodded. "And where's he from?"

"Uh, Albania," I said.

"Really?" Mom's expression suddenly brightened. "That's fascinating. It's such a mysterious country. I can't wait to ask him about it."

"Oh, uh, you can't!" I gasped.

Mom frowned. "Why not?"

"Uh, because that's part of the foreign exchange agreement," I said. "The government of Albania insists on maintaining its secrecy. We're not allowed to ask him anything about his country except what's generally known."

"That's very odd," Mom said.

"I know," I said, "but they insisted. Larry's one of the first exchange students ever to come from Albania. It's really a great honor."

"Well, maybe we could ask him just a few simple questions at dinner," she said.

"Oh, uh, gee," I said, "I forgot to tell you. Cody

and I are taking him to the mall. He's never seen a mall before."

"Well, then we'll see you at dinner tomorrow night."

"But — "

"No buts, sweetheart," Mom said. "If Larry is going to stay with us, the least he can do is join us for dinner."

I could see I wasn't going to get out of it. "Uh, sure. Catch you later." I started out of the kitchen.

"Max?" Mom said.

I stopped. "Yeah?"

"What's with his hair?"

"His hair?"

"It sticks out all over the place. Can't he comb it?"

"Well, you know," I said. "Albania."

Mom nodded. I went upstairs. Great, I thought, now I had to bring Larry to dinner with my parents and the guy was supposed to know something about *Albania!* How was I going to get us out of *that* mess?

I opened the door to my bedroom and went inside. Larry was lying on my bed, reading one of my textbooks. His shoes were off. Boy, he had ugly feet!

"Hello, Max," he said. "Did you know the square root of sixty-four is eight?"

"Uh, yeah."

"And that the War of 1812 was a complete mistake?"

"Uh no, I didn't."

"Photosynthesis is the process by which carbohydrates are formed in the tissues of plants containing chlorophyll," he said.

"That's great, Larry."

He grinned proudly. "I have now read almost all the books in your room."

I felt my jaw drop. *"All of them?"* There weren't really that many, and they were mostly textbooks. But still . . .

"Can we order a pizza?" Larry asked.

"Uh, not tonight," I said. "Cody and I are taking you to the mall."

"The mall?" Larry's forehead wrinkled.

"It's this place with all these stores where kids hang out," I said.

"Hang out of what?" Larry asked.

"It's just an expression," I said. "It means they, uh, just walk around eating and talking."

"I see." Larry nodded. "Do they have pizza there?"

"Sure."

"Good."

A little while later Cody came over with some of Brett's clothes. Larry went into the bathroom to change while Cody and I waited in my bedroom. I noticed that Cody had fixed her hair up and was even wearing a little makeup.

"Hey, you're looking hot," I kidded her.

Cody blushed a little, then quickly changed the subject. "So how's it going?"

"Okay, I guess." I told her how my mother had insisted Larry and I eat dinner with them the next night, and how Larry had read all the books in my room.

"Really?" Cody looked surprised. "Do you think he's smart?"

"Well, Lincoln was no dummy," I said.

The bedroom door opened and Larry stepped out. He was wearing jeans, sneakers, a shirt, and a sweatshirt.

"Larry, you look cool!" Cody gushed.

Larry grinned self-consciously. "Why thank you, ma'am. You look pretty swell yourself."

Cody blushed again.

"What about his hair?" I asked.

"Oh, don't worry, I brought some mousse."

"Where?" Larry looked around quickly.

"Not moose," Cody said, taking a spray can out of her bag. "Mousse. It's for your hair."

Back in my bedroom, Larry sat on the edge of the bed and Cody sprayed on the mousse and fixed up his hair.

"There," she said when she was finished. "Now you look really nice." She turned to me. "What do you think, Max?"

"Frankly, I think he'd look better with a buzz cut," I said.

The mall was about half a mile away, so we walked. Larry got to the first corner and just kept going.

Screeecccch! Beeeeeeep! A car slammed on its brakes and the driver hit the horn. Cody and I grabbed Larry and pulled him back to the sidewalk. We quickly explained about cars and streets and traffic signals.

When the light turned green, we crossed the street. Cody and Larry talked almost all the way to the mall. I couldn't remember the last time Cody was so talkative.

Finally we got there and showed Larry around all the stores. At the pizza place Cody and Larry talked so much that I started to feel a little left out. After that we went into the video arcade. I thought Larry would be into the games, but he just stood there and talked to Cody.

At one point he had to go use the bathroom. Cody watched him walk away with a dreamy look on her face. I stopped in the middle of Suicide Pact and turned to her.

"What's with you?" I asked.

"Huh?" Cody looked surprised.

"You guys haven't stopped talking since we left my house."

"I . . . I guess we have a lot to talk about."

"How can you have a lot to talk about?" I asked. "The guy doesn't remember anything that happened before a couple of days ago. All he knows is what's inside school books."

"Well, that's what we've been talking about," Cody said. "It's interesting to talk to someone who knows so much."

I made a face. "About square roots and photo-synthesis?"

"Yes," Cody said. "Larry's really fascinating."

"Hey, don't forget, four days ago he didn't even know how to use the bathroom."

Cody studied me for a second. "Are you jealous?"

9

Jealous? I didn't know what to say. She'd really caught me off-guard.

Cody smiled. "That's it, isn't it?"

"Jealous of him?" I forced a laugh. "Look, Cody, just because you've finally met a guy who's taller than you and doesn't have a bad case of zits. . . . Don't think that makes me jealous."

"Then what's the problem?"

"*Soooweeeeet!*" Before I could answer, I heard that familiar whistle. Coach Neanderthal stepped into the video arcade carrying a lampshade under his arm. "Hey, kids, I was just walking past and saw you. Having fun?"

"Sure, Coach," I said. "How about you?"

"Just doing some shopping," he said. "It's a real shame we lost to Brunswick, huh?"

Cody and I nodded.

"If only 'Stone Hands' Short hadn't lost the ball with three seconds to go." Neanderthal shook his head.

"It even happens in the pros," I said.

"Maybe you could talk to Ms. Schmidt," said Cody.

The furrows in Coach Neanderthal's sloping forehead deepened. "Why?"

"I think Dave's having a hard time concentrating because he thinks he's going to be Lincoln in her play," Cody explained. "He's terrified of being onstage."

Neanderthal nodded. "I'll talk to her, but I'm not sure it will make a difference now. We have to win almost every game for the rest of the year in order to have a winning season. I guess my one big wish isn't going to come true."

Cody and I gave each other a look. I hated to admit it, but you had to feel bad for the guy. I mean, if *that* was his one big wish.

"Hi, everyone."

We all turned around. Larry was standing there, just back from the bathroom.

Neanderthal gazed up at him with a look of wonder on his face. "Who are you?"

"I'm Larry." He extended his hand. Neanderthal shook it, and made a face.

"Wow! Some handshake!" Neanderthal rubbed his hand. "Larry who?"

"Larry Lincoln," I said. "He's new."

"New?"

"Actually he's Max's cousin," Cody said.

"No, he's a foreign exchange student," I said, giving her a look.

"Well, which are you?" Neanderthal asked Larry.

"Foreign exchange student," Larry said with a smile. "From Albania."

"Where?" Neanderthal asked.

"Albania," Larry said.

"No, I meant, where are you at school?" the coach asked.

"Uh, here," I said.

"Here? You mean, here at Putney?" Neanderthal looked up at Larry as if he was in a daze.

"Is something wrong, Coach?" Cody asked.

"Wrong?" The coach shook his head as if he was trying to snap himself out of a trance. "No, no, nothing." He looked up at Larry again. "What grade are you in, son?"

"Grade?" Larry repeated uncertainly.

"Uh, eighth," I said.

"Eighth," Neanderthal mumbled. "Amazing . . . so, you play basketball?"

Larry shook his head.

Coach Neanderthal's face fell with disappointment. "But you're so tall. Didn't they want you to play at your last school?"

"Not where he comes from, Coach," I tried to explain.

"Don't they play basketball in Albania?" Neanderthal asked Larry. "You must've played a little basketball. Even if it was just in gym."

"Gym?" Larry looked puzzled.

"Uh, they don't have gym in Albania," I said.

"Oh, great!" Coach Neanderthal threw up his hands in despair. "I finally find a guy who could help us have a winning basketball team and he's never played basketball!"

"Well, guess we better get going," I said. "See you at school, Coach."

"Sure, kids." Neanderthal started to turn away. Then he stopped. "Wait!"

"What?" I asked.

"Look." Neanderthal pointed into the video arcade. Right at the entrance was one of those games with the half-size basketballs. "Come with me for a second."

Neanderthal led us over to the game. He fed some coins in and a couple of miniature basketballs came out. He put one into Larry's hand.

"What you want to do is toss this ball through that net." Neanderthal pointed at the miniature net about ten feet away. Larry tossed the ball . . . underhand.

"No, no, not like that. Like this." Neanderthal picked up another ball and shot it into the net.

Larry picked up a ball and shot it. He missed.

"Try again," Neanderthal said.

Larry shot another ball . . . and missed.

"Again," said Neanderthal.

Larry shot. This time the ball fell through the net.

"All right!" Cody clapped her hands.

Neanderthal said, "Again."

Larry shot. The ball went through the net.

Neanderthal grinned.

"Come with me." He led us to the Sports Warehouse store. Inside was a big barrel filled with basketballs. He took two out and handed one to Larry. Then he started to dribble. "Do what I'm doing."

Larry, I mean, Abe, tried to dribble.

"Don't slap it," Neanderthal said. "Just bounce it."

Larry bounced with two hands.

"Try with one hand."

Larry did it.

"Now the other."

Fifteen minutes later, Larry was dribbling up and down the aisles. Neanderthal had a big smile on his face. "The kid learns fast."

Cody and I nodded. We knew that.

Neanderthal clapped his hands together. "Okay, Larry, that's enough!"

Larry dribbled back to us and stood there panting a little.

"I want you three in the gym tomorrow morning at nine o'clock sharp," Neanderthal said.

"But tomorrow's Saturday," I said.

"Listen." Neanderthal pointed a hairy finger at

me. "Our next game is Wednesday. And now that Larry's on the team, we can win."

"But Larry isn't on the team," I said. "He doesn't even go to our school."

Neanderthal looked surprised. "I thought you said he was an exchange student."

"Uh . . ." Gee, I had said that, hadn't I?

"It's a state law that every child under the age of sixteen residing within the district must attend school," Neanderthal said. "You want to be arrested for harboring a truant?"

"We'll be there tomorrow morning, Coach," I said.

Neanderthal smiled. "Great."

10

On the way home, we stopped at Brian's house. I knocked on the front door while Larry and Cody waited on the sidewalk. I didn't want Larry to hear what I was going to say to Brian. I heard someone humming happily to himself on the other side of the door. Then Brian opened it.

"Uh, Max, what're you doing here?" He looked surprised.

"I have to talk to you," I said.

"Uh, er . . ." Brian's eyes darted around.

"Who's at the door, Brian?" his mother called behind him.

"Just some friends, Mom," Brian called back.

Mrs. Dent appeared in the hall. "What do they want?"

"They want to talk, Mom," Brian said.

"Not in the house," Mrs. Dent said. "I just finished vacuuming."

I looked at my watch. It was 8:14 on a Friday

night. I leaned close to Brian. "She *just* finished vacuuming?"

Brian nodded and whispered, "Second time today. Anyway, wait right here."

He closed the door. A few moments later he came out wearing a coat. Meanwhile, out near the street, Larry and Cody were deep in conversation again.

"So, uh, what's up?" Brian asked in a low voice. He seemed a little nervous.

"Larry's on the basketball team," I whispered. "Neanderthal discovered him at the mall."

"Great." Brian nodded. "Maybe we'll win a few games for once."

"Would you get real for a second?" I said. "Larry's not supposed to play basketball. He's supposed to be the sixteenth president of the United States. He's supposed to lead us through the Civil War and free the slaves."

"I don't know what the big rush is," Brian said. "Half a million people died in the Civil War. That's the worst death toll of any war our country ever fought. You could save a lot of lives by not letting it happen."

"What are you talking about?" I asked as I glanced back at Cody and Larry again. "The Civil War *has* to happen, and Larry's got to go back into history. My parents aren't gonna let him live with us forever." I wasn't sure why it was suddenly so important for me to get Larry, I mean,

Abe, back to the 1800s, but it was. I guess I just wanted everything to be normal again.

"So, have you figured out where to send him yet?" I asked.

"Uh, well, I'm having some problems." Brian sort of hemmed and hawed.

"Like what?" I asked.

"There's a lot of disagreement among historians about where Lincoln spent his teenage years." Everyone knows he moved from Kentucky to Indiana when he was seven because his father didn't like the slavery in Kentucky. But at some point they moved to Illinois. Lincoln also made trips to places as far away as New Orleans."

"Can't you just make an educated guess?" I asked.

"And risk sending him to the wrong place at the wrong time?" Brian replied. "Suppose I send him back and he lands in the middle of Sauk Indian territory during a land dispute? How would you like to be responsible for Lincoln getting scalped?"

I looked back at Larry, who was still chatting intensely with Cody. "Couldn't be worse than the haircut he has now. So you figure you'll know by the end of the weekend?"

Brian shook his head. "It's my weekend with Dad. He's picking me up tomorrow morning."

"Well, then when are we gonna send him back?" I asked.

"Look, just give me some more time," Brian said. "As soon as I've got something firm, he's out of here."

"Okay." I glanced out of the corner of my eye at Cody and Larry. "Just make it soon."

11

That night, Larry and I got ready for bed. Larry had been sleeping on the floor for a week, but he didn't seem to mind. Maybe a sleeping bag on a carpeted floor was more comfortable than what he'd slept on back in the 1800s. Anyway, he was already on the floor when I got back from the bathroom. I got into bed and turned off the light.

I usually didn't have any trouble falling asleep, but for some reason that night I lay in bed with my eyes open.

"Max?" Larry said after a while.

"Yeah?"

"Am I really the sixteenth president of the United States?"

"Yeah."

"And it's a very important job?"

"Hey, along with George Washington, you just might be the most important president who ever lived," I said.

"Because I freed the slaves?"

"And kept the country from being divided," I said. "You really changed the course of history. Have you ever looked at a penny?"

"No."

I turned on the light and reached for my jeans, which were lying on the floor. Digging through the pocket, I found a penny and flipped it to him. "That's you, dude."

"I don't have a beard," Larry said.

"Not yet. You will." I switched the light back off.

"So it's very important that I go back," he said.

"Yeah. Otherwise who're they gonna put on all those pennies?"

We both lay in the dark for a while.

"Max?"

"Yeah?"

"Have you known Cody for a long time?"

"Just about my whole life," I said.

"She's very nice."

"Yeah."

"Are all girls today as nice as her?"

"Uh, some are."

"Do they all play basketball?"

"Not many."

"Hmmmm. Good night, Max."

"Yeah, Larry, good night."

*　　*　　*

The next morning it was snowing hard when Cody, Larry, and I left for basketball practice. Unlike the last time, this snow was heavy and wet.

"Oh, man," I groaned. "I hope Neanderthal isn't gonna make us practice for long. If this snow keeps up, I'm gonna have driveways to clear today."

"He can't keep us that long," Cody said. "I have to go visit my grandma in the hospital this afternoon."

When we got to the gym, Ricky Detrich and some of the other players were already there.

"What's goin' on?" Ricky asked. "Last night at ten o'clock I got this call from Neanderthal saying I had to be here this morning. Something about a new center for the team."

"Say hello to Larry," I said, and introduced everyone. Larry shook their hands. Everyone grimaced and rubbed their hands when they were through.

"Who's gonna tell Dave?" Ricky asked.

"That's my problem," Neanderthal said, coming up behind us. "Now start playing three on three. Max takes the ball out first."

I brought the ball out and passed it to Larry. Larry tried to dribble, but the ball bounced off his foot and rolled out of bounds.

Sooooweeeet! Neanderthal put his fingers in his mouth and whistled. "Larry, get over here."

Larry jogged over to the sideline.

"Listen, Larry," Neanderthal said. "You're a big guy. I know I showed you how to dribble last night, but in a game you don't try to dribble, okay?"

Larry nodded. The coach told him to position himself near the basket and either wait for a pass or rebound the ball when someone else took a shot. When the other team had the ball, he would either rebound or block shots.

"Any questions?" Neanderthal asked when he was finished.

"Is it fair?" Larry asked.

"Is what fair?" the coach scowled.

"Boxing out the opponent and blocking shots," Larry said.

"Yes, it is completely fair and by the rules," Coach Neanderthal assured him. "Now let's see what you can do."

On our next possession, Larry positioned himself under the basket and rebounded the ball twice until I managed to put one in. And when the other team brought the ball down the court, Larry stood under the basket and blocked Ricky's shot.

"Way to go!" Coach Neanderthal shouted excitedly on the sideline.

We played for three hours that morning. The snow never let up.

"Wow, am I tired," Cody said as we trudged

home after practice through the newly fallen snow.

"Me, too," I said. "And now I have all those driveways to clear."

"Can I help?" Larry asked.

"Thanks, Larry, but I've got the snowblower," I said.

"Larry," Cody said. "I can't believe how fast you learned the game. By the end of practice, you played as if you'd been a center your whole life."

"Thank you, Cody," Larry said.

It was true. I'd never seen anyone learn the game so quickly. As we passed the public library, I suddenly remembered something. "Wait a minute, guys."

"What is it?' Cody asked.

"I just remembered my parents insisted that Larry and I have dinner with them tonight. They're gonna ask him all kinds of questions about Albania."

Cody looked at the library and back at me. "I could help Larry study for a little while before I go to the hospital."

"Would you?" I said. "Great."

"No problem." Cody and Larry went into the library and I headed home.

I got the snowblower out of the garage, but it took forever to start. Once it did, the work was much slower than last time. The snow was wet and heavy, and the snowblower kept jamming on it. It took more than an hour to do my own drive-way. And I still had five driveways to go.

I always did Cody's driveway after mine. I was halfway through it when *clank!* my snowblower suddenly jammed.

I ran home and got a flashlight and a screw-driver. Then I got down in front of the snowblower with the flashlight and started to probe around the insides with the screwdriver.

"Is it safe to do that while it's running?" some-one asked.

I looked up. Cody and Larry were standing in the snow behind me. They must have just come from the library.

"It looks like it could chop your hands off," Larry said.

"Don't worry, it's in neutral," I said.

"Why don't you turn it off before you go poking around?" asked Cody.

"Normally I would," I said. "But it was really hard to start so I'm gonna let it run."

"Can't you wait until tomorrow to get it fixed?" Cody asked.

"I've got four more driveways to do, Cody. It's Saturday afternoon and people are going to want to get their cars out. If I don't get this thing working, I'm in big trouble."

"What's he doing?" Larry, I mean, Abe, pointed at one of our neighbors, who was shoveling his driveway.

"He's using a shovel," I said.

"Can't we do that?" Larry asked.

I glanced at Cody.

"I'd help you if I could, but I have to go to the hospital with my parents," she said.

"That's okay," I said, then turned to Larry. "You *sure* you want to do this? I mean, you must be pretty tired after that practice."

"I want to help you," Larry said.

"Okay, thanks," I said. "I really appreciate it."

In the next three hours we shoveled the rest of the driveways. I never saw anyone shovel so hard for so long. I tried to keep up with him, but I just couldn't. And the funny thing was, even when I stopped to rest, Larry kept right on shoveling.

"Aren't you tired?" I asked in the middle of the last driveway. My arms were so weary I could hardly lift the snow shovel.

"A little," Larry admitted. "But I'll keep going."

We finished the last driveway just before dinner. When it was time to divide up the money for the work we'd done, I gave Larry what I thought was his share.

"But this is more than half," he said.

"You did more than half the work," I said.

"That's not fair," Larry said, handing some of the money back. "It's not like you didn't try."

"I know, but you still did more work," I said.

"We'll split this evenly," Larry said, giving me some money. "This way there'll be no misunderstandings."

I took the money, but I felt funny. Not so much about the money as about Larry. He just wasn't like any other kid I'd ever known.

12

That evening, my parents actually took time from their tax work to have dinner with Larry and me. Over meat loaf and mashed potatoes, I told them how Coach Neanderthal had made Larry the new center for the Putney basketball team.

"Did you play back in Albania?" my father asked.

"No," Larry said. "We have no gyms in Albania. It is the smallest country on the Balkan Peninsula. Just eleven thousand square miles, or twenty-eight thousand seven hundred and forty-eight square kilometers."

My father glanced at my mother and frowned. "I, er, see."

And I could see that Larry had really studied up on Albania with Cody. Maybe a little *too* well.

"But surely, eleven thousand square miles is large enough for *a few* gyms," my mother said.

"Albania is very mountainous," Larry said.

"The highest mountain is Mount Korab at nine thousand, twenty-six feet, or two thousand seven hundred and fifty-one meters."

"So how do you like it here in Putney?" I asked, hoping to change the subject.

"It is much colder here than in Albania," Larry said. "There we have a more Mediterranean climate. Hot, dry summers and mild, wet winters. Not very much snow, except occasionally at the higher elevations."

"So what did you do in Albania?" my mother asked.

"Most Albanians are descendants of herders," Larry said. "There are two major groups of people. The Ghegs, who live north of the Shkumbin River, and the Tosks, who live south of the river. There are also small amounts of Gypsies, Greeks, and Vlachs, but they amount to no more than three percent of the population."

"Very interesting," said my father. "And where in Albania do you come from?"

"Tirane, the capital, with nearly two hundred thousand inhabitants," Larry said. "Chief exports: tobacco, wine, and asphalt."

"I always wondered where asphalt came from," my father said.

"So tell us about your family," my mother said.

Larry's mouth opened, but nothing came out. I suddenly realized that he and Cody had prepared for Albania, but probably not Larry's family.

"Uh, that's one of the things he's not allowed to talk about," I said.

"Really? Why?" My mother frowned.

"Albania's been a closed country for decades," I said. "They're only now starting to open it, but they're still very private about their personal lives."

"I see." Mom nodded and we ate in silence for a while. Then Larry cleared his throat.

"I would like to thank you for letting me live here and feeding me during my stay," he said.

"We're delighted," my father said.

"Yes, it's no trouble at all," agreed my mother. "But I was wondering, Larry, how long you thought you'd be staying with us."

Larry gave me a quick glance.

"Uh, well, at least until Jake's brother gets better," I said.

"You said he had the measles?" Mom recalled. "I'd imagine he'd be past the contagious stage by now."

"Uh, there were complications," I said.

"Oh, really?" Dad asked.

"What happened?" asked Mom.

"Well, uh, he had measles," I said. "Then he went outside too soon and now he's got pneumonia."

"That's terrible," my father said.

"Yeah, he's in the hospital," I said. "I guess Larry could go stay with Jake if you *really* wanted him to."

"Oh, no," said Mom. "Jake's parents must have enough on their minds. Larry should stay here until things get better."

I couldn't help smiling. Way to go, Mom.

On Monday morning, Cody and I walked to school with Larry. It was an amazingly warm and sunny day for January. Brian almost always went to school before us to work in the computer lab.

"You don't have to be nervous," I assured Larry. "We'll just take you to the principal's office and you'll register. You'll always be in class with Cody or me."

"And I should say I'm an exchange student from Albania?" Larry asked.

"No!" Cody and I both said at the same time.

"Why not?" Larry asked.

"Because there's bound to be someone at school who knows more about Albania than my parents," I said.

"Then what should he say?" Cody asked.

"Uh, say that you're my cousin from Kansas," I said. "You've come to live with us because your whole family was wiped out in a tornado."

"Won't they want his transcripts?" Cody asked.

"Hmmmm." That was a problem. Then I had

an idea. "Tell them it was a really bad tornado. It seriously damaged your school. It'll be weeks before all the paperwork is sorted out."

Cody frowned. "Sounds pretty strange, Max."

"Look, the bottom line is they have to take him," I said. "Remember what Neanderthal said? It's the law."

We got to school. Cody agreed to take Larry to Principal Foote's office while I went to the computer lab to see if Brian had any news.

I found him in the lab alone, staring at a computer screen.

"Hey, Brian," I said, pulling up a seat next to him. On the computer screen were long rows of symbols that looked like gibberish to me. "How was your weekend?"

Brian glanced nervously at me out of the corner of his eye. "Uh, hi, Max. It was okay."

"How come you work on this computer every morning when you have one at home?" I asked.

"Because I can't wait to get out of the house and away from my mother," Brian explained. He pointed at a small box with red lights on it. "See this modem? I use it to hook back into my computer at home. So it's just like being on my computer, only my mother isn't telling me to eat my oatmeal."

"So, any news about Abe?" I asked.

"I, uh, don't know yet," Brian said. "I got home late last night and didn't have time to check my

E-mail. There are still a few important historians I'm waiting to hear from."

"Brian, we have to do something pretty soon or we're never going to get him back where he belongs," I said.

"You think I don't know that?" Brian asked. "You should see what'll happen if Lincoln doesn't go back."

I stared at him for a moment. "You mean, you *know?*"

"Oh, uh, no, no, that's not what I meant," Brian said quickly. "I'm just *imagining* what it would be like."

"Oh, okay," I said. "For a second there I thought maybe you'd figured out some way to connect your computer to your time machine. So you could look into the future and stuff."

For a moment, Brian stared at me wide-eyed. Then he shook his head and snapped out of it. "Ha!" he forced a laugh. "I *wish!*"

"What are you doing?" I pointed at the computer.

"Uh, working on a program for my dad," Brian said. "He wants me to help him set up a desk-top printing operation. He's gonna start his own magazine."

"Oh, yeah? What kind of magazine?"

"Uh, I, er, really don't want to say," Brian said.

Once again, I decided not to push it. Brian's father was sort of a crazy genius type, like Brian, who was always getting involved in bizarre business schemes that always failed.

"Well, I hate to say this, Brian, but don't you think sending Lincoln back in history is more important than helping your father with his magazine?"

"Look, I promise," Brian said. "As soon as I get home this afternoon I'll get back to work on it."

Briinnnnggg! The bell rang and it was time for homeroom to begin. Brian and I left the computer lab and went to Ms. Schmidt's room. Cody was already there.

"How'd it go?" I asked.

"Okay, I guess," she said. "I told the secretary Larry was your cousin from Kansas. Then Mr. Foote took him into his office and shut the door."

I felt a pang of nervousness. "I hope Larry remembers the story."

Dave Short came into the room and slumped down behind his desk with his head in his hands.

"I think Neanderthal must've told him he's being replaced as the center," Cody whispered.

"Poor guy." I felt bad for Dave.

Then Ms. Schmidt came in and started homeroom. She was in the middle of taking attendance when the door opened and Mr. Foote walked in, followed by Larry. Mr. Foote had been the auto shop teacher over at the high school, but they'd phased out his job and made him principal of the

Putney School. He was a short man with a blond crew cut.

"Ms. Schmidt," Mr. Foote said. "I'd like to introduce our newest eighth-grader, Larry Lincoln. He's Max Espy's cousin and he's just transferred in."

Whew! A wave of relief washed through me. Principal Foote had believed the story!

Ms. Schmidt stared at Larry like she was in a daze. "Did you say Larry *Lincoln?*"

Principal Foote nodded. "Just like the president."

"Uh, welcome to the eighth grade, Larry," Ms. Schmidt said, looking at him strangely. "Take a seat and we'll all try to make you feel welcome."

After homeroom, we stayed in our seats for social studies, also with Ms. Schmidt.

"As you know, today's the day I said I'd announce who will play the role of Lincoln in our Presidents' Day play," she said. Once again she gazed for a long time at Larry, then seemed to snap out of it.

"Oh, no," Dave groaned softly and buried his head in his hands.

"One thing I always like to do when a new student comes into school is get them involved immediately," Ms. Schmidt continued. "So I've decided that . . . Larry will play the role of Abraham Lincoln."

Dave looked up with an amazed expression on his face. "Yes!" He pumped his arm triumphantly, then jumped up and went over to Larry's desk.

"Let me shake your hand," Dave said, holding out his hand.

Larry stood up and they shook hands.

"Ow!" Dave rubbed his sore hand. "That's some handshake. But anyway, welcome to Putney School!"

The class laughed.

"All right, Dave, you can go back to your seat now," Ms. Schmidt said with a smile.

Dave sat down and I leaned over to Cody and whispered, "I guess Dave isn't so upset about not being center anymore."

"We'll all work together with Larry, and that way he'll get to know us," Ms. Schmidt said.

A little while later the bell rang and we got up to go to our next class, which was gym.

"Larry, Max, and Brian, would you stay after class for a second?" Ms. Schmidt asked.

We waited until the rest of the class left. Ms. Schmidt gazed at Larry again. "Where did you say you're from?"

"Uh, he's my cousin," I said quickly. "From Kansas."

It seemed like Ms. Schmidt couldn't take her eyes off Larry. "Has anyone ever told you that you look *exactly* like Abraham Lincoln when he was young?"

Larry sort of nodded his head.

"You're not related, are you?"

Larry sort of shrugged.

"Well, it's a truly remarkable coincidence," Ms. Schmidt said. Then she turned to me. "Max, I was wondering if I could ask you a favor. Since Larry is new and he's living with you, would you take some time and show him what we've covered so far this year in English and social studies?"

"Uh, sure," I said.

"Good," Ms. Schmidt said. "Now you better get going or you'll be late. Brian, I want you to stay for a moment."

We went out into the hall and headed for gym. Brian stayed behind to talk to Ms. Schmidt in private. Out in the hallway, Dave was waiting for us.

"Hey, guys," he said with a big smile.

"Hey, Dave," I said a little nervously. I was still worried that he might be mad that Larry had taken his position.

Dave patted Larry on the back. "I just wanted to tell you again how happy I am that you're gonna be Lincoln in the play. I was totally dreading it, you know?"

Larry nodded.

"And I want you to know there are no hard feelings about the basketball team," Dave said as we walked toward the gym. "In fact, now that you're the center, I think I'm going to quit."

"Why?" Larry asked.

"Well, it's too much pressure," Dave said. "Like every time we lose, Coach Neanderthal makes me feel like it's my fault. I really like playing basketball, but I've gotten to the point where I really hate being on the team."

"I'd like you to stay on the team," Larry said.

Dave looked surprised. I was pretty surprised, too.

"Why?" Dave asked.

"Because you like the game and you should be part of it," Larry said. "Besides, I might not be on the team forever."

He was right. I'd completely forgotten that as soon as he went back to the 1800s, we'd need a center again.

"Why not?" Dave asked.

"Well, you never know," Larry said, giving me a wink. "Perhaps you and I could share the position and take turns. I'd be very sad if you didn't get to play because of me."

Dave and I just looked at him in amazement. Usually the *last* thing a player wanted to do was share a position.

"Wow," Dave said. "That's really nice of you. I'll do it."

13

At lunch, Cody and I were sitting near the windows in the cafeteria when Dave and Larry came out of the lunch line carrying trays. The day had gotten warmer and sunnier and the cafeteria windows had been opened slightly to let in the fresh air.

"Hey, guys!" I waved and they joined us.

"So did you guys talk to Neanderthal?" I asked.

"Oh, man, did we," Dave said with a big grin.

"What happened?" asked Cody.

"We went into his office and Larry told him he wanted to share the center's position with me," Dave said. "Well, Neanderthal just about freaked! He couldn't come right out and say that he didn't want me to play, but he kept hinting around that he thought Larry should be the only center."

"So then what?" I asked.

"Finally Larry just laid it on the line," Dave

said. "He told Neanderthal that we either shared the position or he wouldn't play at all."

"Really!?" Cody gazed at Larry with this mushy look on her face.

"This is one stand-up guy," Dave said, slapping Larry on the back. Larry just smiled and shrugged like it was no big deal.

Suddenly we were interrupted by the sounds of an argument coming from outside.

"We were here first!" Ricky was yelling.

"No, we were," Sabrina shouted back.

Outside the window was a spot where the sun had dried up the sidewalk. Ricky and a couple of other guys were there, but so was Sabrina with her girlfriends.

"Look," Ricky yelled. "This is the wall where we always play watermelon, and that's what we're going to play."

"Forget it, Ricky," Sabrina countered. "This is the only dry spot around and we're going to sit outside and get some sun."

"You're such a jerk, Sabrina," Ricky yelled angrily. "The only reason you want to sit here is so that you can ruin our game."

"You're so self-centered," Sabrina shot back. "What makes you think I even care about your game? We've been stuck inside for months. This is the first dry sunny day we've had and we want to be outside."

"Those two never stop fighting," said Dave, shaking his head.

Now Mr. Foote joined them. "All right, kids, what's the problem?"

Sabrina and Ricky both began complaining loudly.

"Whoa!" Mr. Foote raised his hands. "Surely we can find a solution to this. Why don't you take turns?"

"Fine," said Ricky. "We go first."

"No, *we* go first," Sabrina insisted.

"Sabrina, you can go first," Mr. Foote said.

Sabrina stuck out her tongue at Ricky. She and her friends started to settle into the sun.

"How long is she going to get?" Ricky asked.

"Oh, I think ten minutes is fair," Mr. Foote said.

"Ten minutes!" Ricky cried. "There's only fifteen minutes left in the period!"

"Okay, then we'll split the time evenly," Mr. Foote said. "You'll each get, er . . . uh . . ."

Mr. Foote was having trouble dividing fifteen in half.

"Seven and a half minutes," Cody yelled from the window.

"Er, of course, I was just about to say that," Mr. Foote said. "You'll each get seven and a half minutes."

"That's not enough time to play watermelon!" Ricky fumed.

"And it's not enough time to sit outside either," added Sabrina.

"Well, I'm sorry, kids, but it's the best solution I can offer," Mr. Foote said.

"It's not good enough," Sabrina snapped, crossing her arms.

Larry got up from the table and went to the window. "Uh, excuse me, Mr. Foote." Outside, everyone turned and looked at him.

"Yes, Larry?" Mr. Foote said.

"I think I have a solution," Larry said.

Mr. Foote looked surprised. "Like what?"

"Maybe Sabrina and her friends would like to join in the game of watermelon," Larry said. "That way they'll all get to use the space for fifteen minutes."

Sabrina and Ricky gave each other quizzical looks and then nodded. Mr. Foote smiled.

"That was a very good idea, Larry," he said through the window. "I think you may have a future in school administration."

"I'll be sure to consider it, Mr. Foote," Larry said.

Back at the lunch table, Cody turned to me with an astonished look. "Since when does an eighth-grader come up with ideas that a principal can't think of?"

"When he's going to be the sixteenth president of the United States," I replied.

That night, Larry and I went over all the stuff we'd studied so far that year. When we started to study Abraham Lincoln, I felt pretty weird. *Especially* when we got to the part where John Wilkes Booth shot the great president in the head at Ford's Theatre.

Larry read that part, then put down the history book and gazed out my bedroom window into the dark. I didn't know what to say. I mean, what *can* you say to someone who's just read about his own death?

"Abraham Lincoln was a very great man," he said after a while.

"Yeah, he really was," I said.

Larry turned and looked at me. "Did they have pizza in his time?"

"I hate to say this, but I sort of doubt it."

Larry let out a big sigh and shook his head.

14

Wednesday afternoon came. This would be the first game with Larry sharing the center's position with Dave. The game was against Smithtown, a team Putney had not beaten in twenty-five years. Before the game, Coach Neanderthal gathered us together in the hall outside the locker room for a pep talk. He used to give the pep talks in the boys' locker room, but now that Cody was on the team, we had to meet in a neutral place. He stood before us in his blue warm-up suit with his basketball under his arm.

"Now remember, boys," He started to say.

"Ahem." Cody cleared her throat.

"Uh, remember boys and girl," Neanderthal said. "Our record is one win and three losses. In order for us to have a winning season this year we have to win almost every remaining game. Now, get out there and mash 'em!"

The game was really close. Larry played out of his mind, blocking shots and grabbing rebounds.

Neanderthal was really reluctant to take him off the court and put Dave in, but Larry insisted.

The amazing thing was that Dave also had a great game. He scored six points and didn't lose the ball once! With less than a minute to go the score was tied 42–42. In front of our bench Neanderthal's collar was pulled open and his warm-up suit had big sweat stains under the armpits. He screamed orders from the sideline, but out on the court the roar of the crowd was so great we could hardly hear him. We could only see him waving his arms and gesturing wildly.

"Got the feeling he really wants to win this one?" I said to Cody as we waited for a guy on the Smithtown team to shoot a free throw.

"You'd think his life depended on it," she said, wiping the sweat off her forehead.

The Smithtown guy sank his free throw to make the score 43–42. I took the ball out and started to dribble down the court. I spun away from the opposing guard and drew Smithtown's center away from Larry, who cut under the net. I passed the ball to him, and he started to go back door. It was going to be an easy two points, and then suddenly . . .

Larry stopped and handed the ball to the referee! The ref looked shocked, but he blew his whistle and handed the ball to one of the Smithtown players.

"Wait a minute! Time out! Time out!" Neanderthal waved his arms and ran out onto the court.

"My man had the ball!" he shouted excitedly at the ref as we all gathered around. "What happened?"

"He gave me the ball," the ref replied.

"What!?" Coach Neanderthal looked like he was going to have a heart attack. "Why?"

"He said he stepped on the line."

"Huh?" The coach turned and gave Larry a puzzled look.

"It's true," Larry said.

"Wait a minute." Coach Neanderthal turned back to the ref. "Did you see him step on the line?"

"No," the ref said. "But he said he did so I believe him."

"But you didn't see it," the coach said. "You didn't call it."

"But I did," Larry said.

"Will you stay out of this!" Coach Neanderthal screamed at him.

"But — " Larry started to argue.

"Max!" the coach yelled at me and I knew what he wanted. I took Larry by the arm and led him away. Meanwhile, Coach Neanderthal shouted and waved his hands at the ref.

"I don't understand what the problem is," Larry said.

"Look," I said. "You know and I know you stepped on the line. But if the ref doesn't see it, it doesn't matter."

"It does to me," Larry said.

Now Coach Neanderthal came over. His face was so red he looked like he might explode at any moment. "Are you crazy, Larry?" he yelled. "There's less than a minute left in the game! The other team's winning by one point! Why in the world did you tell the ref you stepped on the line?"

"Because it's the truth," Larry replied.

Coach Neanderthal stared at him in disbelief. "The truth? What does *that* have to do with anything?"

"Everything," Larry said.

Cody looked at me with wide, astonished eyes.

"Hey," I said with a shrug. "They did call him Honest Abe."

The game resumed and we managed to tie the score and send it into overtime. Then we wound up winning by three points. In a flash, everyone forgot what Larry had done. The only thing that mattered was that we'd beaten Smithtown for the first time in twenty-five years.

15

In the weeks that followed, Larry began to fit into the eighth grade. We got so used to him that I almost forgot he was supposed to go back in history and be Abraham Lincoln. At home my mom asked a couple of times how much longer he was going to stay, but I told her Jake's brother's condition had gotten worse. In fact, now he was in the hospital on life-support systems. In the meantime Larry did the dishes and took out the garbage at night. Even my parents were getting used to him.

With every practice and every game Larry became a better basketball player. But he never bragged about it. Instead he was sort of modest. He seemed pretty friendly most of the time, but sometimes he also got very quiet and seemed a little sad.

With him on the team, we won three of our next five games for a record of five wins and five losses.

Meanwhile, our class had been rehearsing for

the Presidents' Day play. We had made a set and props and costumes, and wrote a script using the questions we'd come up with. In addition to Larry playing Lincoln, other kids played Robert E. Lee, Harriet Beecher Stowe, Ulysses S. Grant, General Stonewall Jackson, and Mary Lincoln.

Since the whole seventh grade was only twenty-one kids, we always invited them to be the audience. Cody handed out playbills and I ran the video camera. Ms. Schmidt sat with us, with a copy of the script in her lap.

"Notice anything strange?" Cody whispered to me.

I looked around the room. "Brian's not here."

"He *never* misses school," she whispered. For Brian, staying home meant spending the day with his mother.

"He must be really sick," I whispered.

The play started with Larry coming into the room. He was wearing a long, dark coat, a fake beard, and a tall top hat.

Next to me, Ms. Schmidt caught her breath and put her hand on her chest. "He looks so real," she whispered in a gasp.

Cody and I glanced at each other. He did look real. Real enough to remind us that he wasn't supposed to be a student at Putney School.

Suddenly the classroom door opened and there was Brian! He was wearing a white wig, a black and gold military jacket with fringed gold epaulets, riding breeches, and high leather boots.

"What's going on?" I asked.

"This isn't in the script," Cody said.

We both turned to Ms. Schmidt, but she didn't look surprised at all. She was smiling.

"Brian and I decided to surprise everyone," she whispered.

"Are you Abe Lincoln?" Brian asked Larry.

"Yes," said Larry. "I am the sixteenth president of the United States, the one known as Honest Abe and the Great Emancipator. I fought to keep our country whole, and freed the slaves. And who are you?"

"I am George Washington, the first President of the United States," Brian replied. "The one called the Father of His Country, who led the fight for freedom from English rule. I also presided over the creation of the United States Constitution, the rules upon which this great nation was founded."

"Did you not own more than two hundred slaves?" Larry asked.

"It was a common practice in my time," Brian defended himself. "We treated them well, and they were all given their freedom after my death. Besides, you take too much credit for things you didn't do."

"I beg your pardon," Larry sputtered.

"You claim you freed the slaves," Brian said. "But in truth all you did was issue that flimsy Emancipation Proclamation, which everyone ignored."

"But it led the way for the Thirteenth Amendment," Larry insisted. "And that made all men free."

"The Thirteenth Amendment wasn't passed until nine months after your death," Brian pointed out.

"Oh, yeah?" Larry shot back angrily. "Well, how many native American Indians did you drive from their rightful lands?"

"You fought the Indians too!" Brian replied.

"Never touched one!" Larry insisted.

"But not for lack of trying!" Brian yelled. "You were captain of a company of riflemen whose job was to drive the Sauk and Fox Indians from their lands. Did you not state later that being made captain gave you great pleasure?"

"Yes!" Larry retorted. "Being made captain did give me pleasure, but not driving away Indians. And while we're on the topic of the truth, is it not true that you never did throw that silver dollar across the Rappahannock River?"

"That was just a silly story Parson Weems made up," Brian allowed. "But the truth is, I had the strength and could have if I'd wanted to."

"Hogwash!" Larry shot back. "What would a

pampered product of the privileged class like you know about strength?"

Ms. Schmidt looked down at the papers in her lap and shook her head. "This isn't the direction we agreed to go in," she whispered.

Meanwhile, in the front of the classroom, Brian raised his fists. "Look who's talking, you skinny beanpole country bumpkin."

Larry raised *his* fists. "I may be a country bumpkin, but I was a champion rail splitter in my day!"

"Boys!" Ms. Schmidt called nervously. "Please, this is only a play."

"Gentlemen!" Now Ricky, dressed as Ulysses S. Grant, stepped between them. "Is this any way for great men to act?"

"Look who's talking!" Larry glowered at him. "A drunken stooge whose greatest victories were planned by other generals!"

Ms. Schmidt kept shaking her head and pointing down at the script. "None of this is what we agreed on."

"How dare you?" Ricky gasped. "I was the eighteenth president of the United States."

"You were nothing but a pawn to self-serving politicians!" Larry yelled at him.

"Your presidency was utter disgrace and dishonesty!" Brian shouted.

The next thing we knew, they *both* grabbed

Ricky and pushed him over toward the seventh-graders. *Crash!* Ricky went flying into the seats.

Larry and Brian faced each other again.

"And as for you . . ." Larry rolled up his sleeves. "I could wield an axe twice as well as you with one hand tied behind my back!"

"All brawn and no brain," Brian snapped.

"No brain?" Larry growled. "You're the one who could hardly read and was a terrible speller. That's why you had Thomas Jefferson and Alexander Hamilton. They did all your thinking for you."

"Why, you!" Brian ripped off his jacket and lunged at Larry, who quickly got him in a headlock.

"Boys!" Ms. Schmidt jumped up and shouted.

"Unh!" "Ooof!" Crash! Grunting and wrestling, Larry and Brian crashed through the props and set.

"Stop them!" Ms. Schmidt shouted.

A bunch of us grabbed them and pulled them apart.

"You're nothing but a big stupid aristocratic figurehead!" Larry shouted at Brian as he struggled to get out of our grip.

"And you're just a power-hungry fool who takes credit for things you didn't do!" Brian shouted back.

We finally got Larry and Brian separated. Ms. Schmidt hurried to the front of the classroom and stood amid the shredded remains of the set and the broken props as she addressed the seventh-graders.

"And, uh, that ends our play, I think," she said.

"Great!" "Awesome!" "Bravo!" The seventh grade stood up and cheered.

"That was the best play we ever saw!" someone shouted.

"Yeah," said another kid. "When does round two begin?"

Even the seventh-grade teachers were impressed.

"That was very enlightening," said one.

"Much better than the last play you did," said another.

The seventh grade left the classroom. Ms. Schmidt turned to Larry and Brian, who'd both calmed down.

"What in the world got into you two?" she asked angrily.

Larry and Brian both shrugged sheepishly. Ms. Schmidt focused on Larry. "If I didn't know better, I would swear you were Abraham Lincoln himself."

Cody and I gave each other knowing looks. I don't know what she was thinking, but as far as I was concerned, it was time to get serious about sending Abe Lincoln back where he belonged.

16

At lunchtime I came out of the lunch line and looked for Brian. Cody and Larry were already sitting off by themselves, deep in conversation. I'd given up trying to figure out what they could spend so much time talking about. All I knew was that every time Cody was around Larry, she got that goofy faraway look on her face.

I found Brian sitting alone near the windows. I put my tray down next to his. He looked up.

"Oh, hi, Max," he said, sounding a little nervous.

"Hi, Brian," I said. "That was a big surprise this morning."

Brian grinned. "It was really Ms. Schmidt's idea. We've been planning it for a couple weeks."

"And what about sending Larry back in time?" I asked. "Don't tell me you're still waiting to hear from historians."

Brian looked around and then leaned toward me. "Let me ask you something, Max," he said in a low voice. "Do you *really* think the Civil War was necessary? I mean, except for the rebel flag and some cool memorabilia, what good was it?"

I looked at him like he was crazy. "It prevented the country from being divided."

"So what's so bad about being divided?" Brian asked. "Look at North and South Korea, North and South America, and North and South Dakota. You don't see them complaining."

"North and South Dakota are states, flea brain," I said.

"Okay, but you get the point," Brian said. "Half a million people got killed. Maybe we'd be better off without it."

I squinted at him. "What are you getting at?"

Brian leaned closer. "How'd you like to be a millionaire?" he asked.

"What are you talking about?" I asked.

"Suppose I told you that if Larry doesn't go back to the 1800s it means that you become rich?"

"How do you know *that?*"

Brian shrugged. "Take my word, Max. I know."

"Are you crazy?" I asked.

"Just think about it," he said, getting up. "I've gotta go to the library. Catch you later."

I watched Brian take his tray over to the tray-return. No Civil War? I'd become rich? How could he know stuff like that? Then it hit me. The time machine . . . his computer . . . maybe Brian *had* figured out a way to tell the future!

I quickly finished lunch and went over to Cody and Larry. They were sitting across from each other, with their heads leaning inward, talking so low that I couldn't hear what they were saying. Every once in a while Cody would giggle and Larry would sort of beam. It was just about enough to make me sick.

"Uh, I hate to interrupt," I said.

They both looked up. "Oh, hi, Max," Cody said, looking a little embarrassed.

"Listen, Cody, you think I could talk to you for a second?"

"Oh, uh . . ." Cody gave Larry a look, like she wanted to make sure it was okay with him. Larry nodded and got up, picking up both their trays.

"Why don't you talk while I take the trays back?" he said.

He left and I sat down. "I think we have a problem."

Cody frowned. "What?"

"I don't think Brian wants to send Larry back," I said. "I'm not sure why, but I definitely get the feeling he wants him to stay here."

Cody gazed across the cafeteria at Larry and nodded. "Maybe he should."

"Cody!" I reached for her arm and shook it. "Do you want to totally mess up history?"

"Well, no. . . ." She was still giving Larry that wistful look.

"What do you see in that guy?" I asked. "He's bony and ugly and he has terrible hair."

"He has character," Cody said with a sigh. "And great inner fortitude."

"Since when is a crush enough of a reason to completely change the course of history?" I asked.

Cody gave me a surprised look.

"Oh, come on," I said. "I've seen the way you act around him. You get totally mushy."

Cody's face turned red.

"Look, all I'm saying is we have to do what's right," I said.

Cody nodded slowly. "How do you know Brian doesn't want to send Larry back?"

I explained how Brian was stalling and how he gave me his word that I'd be rich.

"How could he know *that?*" Cody scowled.

"I'm not sure," I said. "But I think I know how we can find out."

17

I led Cody down to the computer lab. Since it was lunchtime, the lab was empty. I sat down in front of the computer Brian always used and pointed at the modem.

"Brian uses this to call into his computer at home," I explained. "Let's see what happens if I pull up the communications program."

I got the program on the screen, and there was Brian's number. A few moments later, I'd connected to Brian's computer at home.

"But what's the point?" Cody asked as a bunch of icons appeared on the screen.

"*That's* the point," I said, pointing at an icon that said TIME MACHINE. "Brian's figured out a way to connect his computer to his time machine."

Next I found a program of history models. According to their dates, the most recent one was without Abe Lincoln.

"This is the one Brian's been using," I said. Data

began scrolling up the screen. "Look at this! There's no Civil War. The United States gets divided into the Union States and the Confederate States. Slavery continues in the Confederate States."

"Wait a minute!" Cody gasped. "If there's no Civil War, then my great-great-great-grandmother might never have met my great-great-great-grandfather."

"Let's check," I said. I brought the "No Abe Lincoln" model to the present and entered Cody's name, address, and social security number.

INDIVIDUAL DOES NOT EXIST flashed on the screen.

"Oh, no!" cried Cody. "I won't exist!"

"Let's see if Brian was telling the truth about me getting rich," I said. I entered my name, address, and social security number into the computer.

A second later my name appeared on the screen along with some vital statistics such as age, physical description, address, and net worth.

"Ten million dollars!" I cried. "I'm rich, Cody!"

"Only if I don't exist," she muttered and scrolled down the screen to:

Occupation: Invalid

Source of Income: $10 million damage settlement as result of a legal suit filed

101

against the Acme Snowblower corpora-
tion after losing both hands in snow-
blower accident.

"There you go," Cody said with a smile. "You'll be rich, but you won't have any hands."

"Just my luck," I grumbled and typed some more.

"What are you doing now?" Cody asked nervously.

"I want to see what happens to Brian in this model," I said. A moment later Brian's information came up on the screen.

Occupation: Playboy who spends his
time counting money while surrounded
by beautiful women.

Source of Income: Upon graduation
from high school will inherit father's
publishing and entertainment empire.

I leaned back and shook my head. "I should have known."

"You think Brian knows this?" Cody asked.

"Of course he does," I said as I scrolled to the end of the file. "That's why he doesn't want to send Larry back."

We got to the end of the file. There in big block letters was the following message:

**IMPORTANT!
UNLESS PRESENT CIRCUMSTANCES ARE
RETURNED TO THEIR ORIGINAL ORDER,
THIS MODEL WILL GO INTO EFFECT
WORLDWIDE AT 4 P.M. ON
FRIDAY, FEBRUARY 26.**

"That's tomorrow!" I gasped.

Cody's eyes narrowed. "Where's Brian?"

"He said he was going to the library."

Cody stormed out of the computer lab with her hands balled into fists.

"Cody!" I shouted, jumping up and racing after her. "Wait!"

18

By the time I got to the library, Cody was standing over Brian, who was cowering at a table.

"I can't believe you'd do that to me!" she yelled.

"Hey, look at the bright side," Brian whimpered. "After tomorrow you won't have to go to school anymore."

"Because I won't exist," Cody replied angrily.

Brian turned and gave me a hopeful look. "I guess you found out how you'll get rich. So what do you think?"

"About losing both hands?" I asked incredulously. "Check in with reality, bonehead."

"It doesn't have to be all that bad," Brian said. "They're doing wonderful things with prosthetics these days."

"You're sick," I said.

"Okay, listen," Cody said. "Today after school we're sending Larry back."

"But tomorrow's the big game against Plainview," Brian said. "If we win it'll be our first winning season in nearly thirty years. Can't you wait until after that?"

"I won't be *here* if I wait until after that," Cody said. "We're doing it today, right after school. Max, don't you have a study hall with Larry last period?"

"Yeah."

"Maybe you could tell him then."

"What about basketball practice?" I asked.

"We'll be late," Cody said.

Larry was already in study hall when I got there. With a heavy heart, I sat down next to him. Larry looked up and smiled. "Hey, Max."

"Hey, Larry." I felt terrible about breaking the news to him.

"Something wrong?" Larry asked, studying my face.

"Today's the day, Larry," I said. "We have to send you back."

A pained look came across his face. "Really?"

"Yeah." Then I explained how the country would be divided forever, and slavery would continue, and I'd lose my hands and Cody would never exist if he didn't go back.

Larry nodded slowly. "I was afraid something like that might happen."

*　　*　　*

As soon as the last bell rang, Cody and I hurried to our lockers where we met Larry. We'd already agreed with Brian that we'd meet at the front door and all walk home together.

"Okay, guys," I said as I pulled on my jacket and slammed my locker. "Let's go."

We started walking down the hall. Suddenly, from behind us, someone shouted "Stop!"

We spun around. Coach Neanderthal was jogging toward us.

"Where do you think you're going?" he asked, panting for breath.

Cody and I gave each other nervous looks.

"Uh, we were just going out to get some fresh air," Cody said quickly.

"We'll be back in a minute, Coach," I said. "We won't miss practice."

"Forget it." Coach Neanderthal shook his head. "I want all of you in the gym, pronto. We have one game left this year, and if we win it we'll have our first winning season ever. I'm not taking any chances. Now, come on, you three, into the gym."

Larry gave us a helpless look and started to follow the coach back toward the gym. Cody and I fell slightly behind.

"Talk about bad luck," I whispered. "I can't believe he caught us."

"Hmmm." Cody just pursed her lips.

"What are we gonna do?" I asked.

"We'll have to wait until after practice," Cody whispered.

We went through a regular practice. Cody and I both had a hard time concentrating on basketball. I think we were too worried about what would happen if we didn't get Larry back in time.

Soooooweeeeeet! At the end of practice, Coach Neanderthal stuck his fingers in his mouth and whistled. "Okay, boys . . ."

"Ahem." Cody cleared her throat.

"Uh, boys and girl," the coach corrected himself. "Practice is over. Larry front and center."

Cody frowned at me. "Now what?"

"I'll find out in the locker room while we change," I said. I went into the boys' locker room and Cody went into the girls'.

A few moments later Larry came in.

"So what did Neanderthal want?" I asked.

"He wants me to stay at his house tonight," Larry said. "I tried to tell him it wasn't necessary, but he insisted."

"Did he tell you why?" I asked.

Larry shook his head.

"I guess this next game is so important that he just doesn't want to take any risks," Dave said.

Ricky grinned. "Does he think someone's going to kidnap Larry on the way home tonight?"

You never know, I couldn't help thinking.

A little while later I met Cody outside the gym and we started to walk home in the dark. As we walked, I told her that Neanderthal had insisted that Larry stay at his house that night.

"You think he knows?" I asked.

"Of course he knows," Cody said. "Brian must have tipped him off. I can't believe he'd do that to me, just so he could be rich and surrounded by beautiful women. Do you believe it, Max?"

"Well . . . I have to admit it sounds kind of tempting."

Cody glared at me. "Thanks, *friend*." Her voice was heaped with sarcasm.

"Hey, I'd never do that to you," I said. "I just want to know what we're gonna do now."

"I know what *you* can do," Cody grumbled.

"What?"

"Get ready for life with no hands."

19

I got home and went into the kitchen. Both of my parents were sitting there, but the kitchen table wasn't covered with papers. It was bare. And Mom and Dad were staring at me.

"Uh, hi," I said nervously. It was pretty obvious that something was going on.

"Have a seat, Max," my father said.

Now I knew I was in trouble. I sat down.

"I ran into Jake's father this morning," my father said.

Oh-oh.

"Jake's little brother never had the measles," Dad said. "He never had pneumonia and he most certainly wasn't on life-support in the hospital."

What else could I do but nod?

"I also had a conversation with Ellen Brown today," Mom said. "She's involved with the student exchange program. She told me there is no exchange program with Albania and that as far as she knew, there were no students from Albania in our district."

"Would you mind explaining all this?" my father said.

"It was all a lie," I said.

My parents looked at me blankly.

"We don't understand," Mom said.

"It was a lie," I said again. "The problem is, if I told you the truth, you'd never believe me."

"Try us," my father said.

I tried.

I got sent to my room for the rest of the night.

I knew they wouldn't believe me.

Later, I was just falling asleep when the phone rang.

"Hello?" I answered, feeling sort of groggy.

"Hi." It was Cody.

"Oh, hi, what's up?"

"I just figured out what we have to do."

"Really live it up tomorrow?" I guessed.

"No," Cody said. "We have to tell Coach Neanderthal the truth."

"I thought Brian already did," I said.

"I doubt it," Cody said. "Coming from Brian, Neanderthal would never believe it. He probably made up some story about kids from Plainview wanting to kidnap Larry or something like that."

"Well, if he wouldn't believe the truth from Brian, why would he believe it from us?" I asked.

"Because we're not Brian," Cody said.

"You can't be serious, Cody. The only thing Neanderthal wants in life is to retire with a winning season. He'd practically kill for it."

"When we explain that it'll mean you'll have no hands and I'll cease to exist, I bet he'll listen to us," Cody said.

Lying in my bed, I let out a big sigh and shook my head. "Don't you have any better ideas?"

"No."

20

The next morning was Friday, February 26, the last day of the United States as we knew it, the last day of my life with hands, and the last day of Cody's life, period.

In homeroom, Ms. Schmidt called attendance. Brian was absent.

"I knew it," Cody whispered. "He's pretending to be sick. He's going to stay away until I disappear and you lose your hands. He's such a chicken."

As soon as homeroom was over, Cody and I headed for the gym. We found Coach Neanderthal in his office.

"Cody, Max, what's up?" he asked. "Ready for the big game this afternoon?"

"No," Cody said. Then she explained the whole story of how I accidentally brought Abraham Lincoln into the present. And how at 4 P.M. that afternoon the course of history would change completely and forever.

The furrows in Coach Neanderthal's broad forehead deepened. "Are you kids feeling all right?"

"Yes, Coach," Cody answered.

I nodded.

"You haven't been fooling around with anything illegal, have you?"

Cody and I shook our heads vigorously.

"You just expect me to believe that Larry is President Lincoln brought here from the past by a time machine in Brian's closet?" Coach Neanderthal asked.

"You *have* to believe it," Cody insisted. "If we don't put him back where he belongs it's going to change the course of history."

"You're telling me," replied the coach. "I'll finally have a winning season!" Then he leaned across the desk toward us. "Listen, I don't know what's gotten into you two, but there's no way I'm going to let you take Larry *anywhere* until after the game this afternoon."

"But by then it'll be too late!" Cody gasped. "History will change. The country will split in half. Max will lose his hands, and I'll disappear altogether."

"I'll miss you, Cody," Coach Neanderthal said, leaning back in his chair. "Now get out of my office and don't you dare go near my star player."

"But Coach — " Cody gasped.

"I said, get out!" Coach Neanderthal shouted.

"I'm going to retire with a winning season if it's the last thing I do. And I'm not gonna let a couple of eighth-graders with a loony story about changing history stop me."

Cody and I left the gym. I could see that she was really down.

"I'm really sorry, Cody," I said as we walked down the hall. "If I hadn't pushed the wrong button on Brian's computer this never would have happened."

"It's not your fault," Cody said. "You didn't do it on purpose."

"Maybe it won't be as bad as you think," I said. "I mean, once you're gone, maybe you'll never know you were ever here."

Cody gave me a look that would have melted Antarctica.

"On the other hand," I quickly added, "it would be nice if you could stay around."

"Cody? Max?" Ms. Schmidt came to the doorway of her room as we passed in the hall. "Could you come in here, please?"

Cody and I went in and Ms. Schmidt closed the door behind us. "Have a seat, kids," she said. Her usual smile was gone. She looked and sounded serious as she stood in front of us and crossed her arms.

"What do you know about Larry?" she asked.

Cody and I looked at each other and then stared back at her, speechless.

"Uh, what do *you* know, Ms. Schmidt?" Cody finally asked.

"I know that his name, appearance, and personality are almost exactly like those of President Lincoln in his early years," she said. "I've also spoken to your mother, Max. And I know he is neither an Albanian exchange student nor your cousin from Kansas. In fact, nobody in this entire town knows who he is or where he came from."

I slid down a little in my seat. Cody swallowed.

"Now, I find this all quite difficult to comprehend," Ms. Schmidt said. "But since you two seem to know Larry best, I was wondering if you could help me understand what's going on."

For the next twenty minutes, Cody and I explained what had happened since the day of the brownout. We took her to the computer lab and logged into Brian's computer at home. I even offered to take her to Brian's house to show her the time machine. By the time we had finished, Ms. Schmidt was no longer standing. She was sitting, looking like she'd gotten the wind knocked out of her.

"That is the most unbelievable story I have ever heard," she said.

"You're telling us," Cody said.

"The *entire* history of the United States is about to change?" Ms. Schmidt said in amazement.

"And you might not even be part of it anymore when it does," Cody said.

"Forget about me," Ms. Schmidt said. "Think of all the great plays, think of all the great literature that might not have been written. And *you*, Cody. It's terribly unfair."

Cody and I nodded.

"And you're certain you can get Larry back to the past?" she asked.

"We're not certain of anything," I said.

"But it's the only chance we've got," added Cody.

Ms. Schmidt got up and went to the window. She stared out of it, tugging at a short lock of hair, lost in thought. Then she turned back. "You said Brian won't inherit the publishing empire unless he graduates from high school?"

"That's what it said."

"All right." Ms. Schmidt smiled. "I think I know what to do. Cody, you get Larry while I go through the costume closet. Max, go find Brian and tell him I have to see him right now."

"I can't," I said. "Brian's not here."

"Not here?" Ms. Schmidt's jaw dropped. "Where is he?"

"We think he's home, pretending to be sick."

Ms. Schmidt turned to me. "Max, you have to sneak out of school and get him."

21

I snuck out of school and ran all the way to Brian's house. When I got there, I knocked on the door.

No one answered.

"Come on, Brian!" I shouted and knocked harder. "Open up! I know you're in there!"

I kept knocking until the door swung open. Brian was wearing a blue bathrobe.

"Cool it, Max, you'll get fingerprints on the door," he said. "Why aren't you in school, anyway?"

"I could ask you the same question," I said.

"I'm sick," Brian said.

"Yeah, right," I said. "Listen, you have to get dressed and come to school. Ms. Schmidt wants to see you."

"What about?" he asked.

"Your future."

"But I can't go to school," Brian said.

"Where's your mom?" I asked.

"She went to the store to buy vacuum cleaner bags and soap," Brian said.

"Well, you either get dressed and come to school right now, or I'm going to stomp around your whole house *with my shoes on!*" I told him.

"No!" Brian gasped. He tried to slam the door, but I stuck my foot in the way and pushed it open. Brian held out his hands to stop me.

"No, don't, please!" he gasped.

"Two minutes," I said.

Brian turned and dashed upstairs.

When we got back to school, Cody and Ms. Schmidt were standing in the hallway outside her room.

"Is Larry really Abraham Lincoln?" Ms. Schmidt asked Brian.

"Uh . . ." Brian glanced nervously at Cody and me.

"Is it true that Cody will cease to exist and Max will lose his hands if we don't send Larry back in time by four o'clock today?" Ms. Schmidt asked.

"Uh . . ." Brian swallowed.

"Let me tell you something." Ms. Schmidt pointed a finger at him. "According to your father's will, you have to graduate high school before you can inherit his publishing empire. If Cody disappears at four o'clock, I promise that I will see to it that you *never ever* graduate high school."

Brian's face fell. "Aw, Ms. Schmidt, come on."

Ms. Schmidt shook her head and looked disgusted. "I'm very disappointed in you, Brian."

"Where's Larry?" I asked.

Before Ms. Schmidt could answer, a voice inside the room said, "I'm ready."

"Let's go," Ms. Schmidt said. She opened the door and we went in.

I stepped into the room and felt my jaw drop. Larry was wearing a red dress, a blond wig, and makeup. He looked like the tallest, and ugliest, woman I'd ever seen!

"Doesn't he look wonderful?" Ms. Schmidt asked, giving me a big wink that Larry couldn't see.

"Oh, uh, yeah, sure, great," I managed to say. The dress Larry was wearing was meant to be full-length on girls, but it barely reached his knees. From there down were his hairy legs disappearing into scuffed basketball shoes.

"Are you *sure* I need to wear this outfit, Ms. Schmidt?" Larry asked uncomfortably.

"Yes," our teacher replied. "It's absolutely imperative. And whatever you do, you mustn't let Coach Neanderthal see you." Ms. Schmidt turned to me. "Check the hall, Max."

"Okay." I peeked out into the hall.

"How's it look?" Cody asked.

"Coast is clear," I said.

"You, Brian, and Cody walk Larry out the front entrance," Ms. Schmidt said. "I'll go get my car and meet you there."

Cody and I stepped out into the hall with Larry and Brian and started to walk. Except for a couple of little kids who gave Larry funny looks, we didn't see anyone. But just as we reached the lobby, the door to the school office opened and Principal Foote stepped out.

"Oh, kids, hold up." He waved at us and came over, looking curiously at Larry.

"I didn't know you had a guest today," Mr. Foote said.

"Er, uh, yes," I said nervously. "This is my cousin, uh, visiting from er, Alaska."

"I never knew you had so many cousins, Max," Mr. Foote said, and offered his hand to Larry. "Hello."

Larry was about to shake it when I remembered how hard he shook, and jumped in between them.

"Uh, I wouldn't do that, Mr. Foote," I said.

"Not shake hands?" Mr. Foote frowned. "Why not?"

"Uh, because it means something different in Alaska than it means here," I said.

"It does?" Mr. Foote looked puzzled. "Like what?"

"It means, 'I want to kiss you.' "

Mr. Foote looked up at Larry in his wig. "Well, in that case . . ."

Suddenly I felt a sharp nudge in my ribs. "Max!" Cody hissed.

"Huh?" I turned. Cody was motioning down the hallway. At the far end of the hall I saw Coach Neanderthal coming toward us.

"Uh-oh, gotta skate, Mr. Foote," I gasped, tugging Brian with me. Cody grabbed Larry.

"But school's not over," Mr. Foote said.

"Ms. Schmidt is taking us somewhere," Cody said, pushing open the front door and pointing at Ms. Schmidt's car.

"Hey, wait!" Down the hall Coach Neanderthal shouted and started to run toward us.

"Let's go!" I yelled.

22

We ran out the doors, dragging Larry and Brian with us. Behind us I saw Coach Neanderthal run up to Mr. Foote and start to wave his hands excitedly.

"The coach knows!" I yelled as we jumped into Ms. Schmidt's car.

"Step on it!" Cody shouted.

Ms. Schmidt took off. Through the back window we watched Coach Neanderthal run out to the parking lot and jump in his car.

"He's following us!" I yelled.

"Oh, how exciting!" Ms. Schmidt gasped. "A car chase!"

"It's not going to be exciting if he catches us," Cody yelled.

Luckily we didn't have far to go. A few minutes later Ms. Schmidt skidded to a stop in front of Brian's house.

I jumped out of the front seat and helped Cody get Larry and Brian out of the back.

"What should I do?" Ms. Schmidt asked.

"Try to stop Neanderthal," Cody yelled.

We ran up to the front door and rang the bell.

Mrs. Dent opened the door and stared at us. Then her eyes went to Brian. "Where have you been? I got home and you weren't here. I've been so worried."

"I, uh, had to go to school," Brian said.

"Listen, Mrs. Dent," I said urgently. "We have to come in."

Mrs. Dent instantly looked down at our feet. "All of you?"

"Yes," I said. "Quick, everybody, take off your shoes."

While we took off our shoes, Mrs. Dent turned to Brian. "What is this all about, Brian?"

"Uh, it's hard to explain, Mom," Brian said meekly.

"Well, I'm going to expect an explanation later," his mother grumbled.

We'd just gotten our shoes off when Neanderthal skidded to a stop at the curb. "Stop them!" he shouted.

"Now, you're being extremely selfish, Neal," Ms. Schmidt said, blocking his path.

"What's *that* all about?" Mrs. Dent asked.

"They're having a personal problem," I said, starting into the house.

"Stop!" Mrs. Dent raised her arm. "You have

to wash your hands. Then stay on the plastic runner and go only to Brian's room."

"You bet," I said.

"Wait!" Mrs. Dent said again.

"Think of history!" Ms. Schmidt shouted as she struggled with Neanderthal behind us.

"The heck with history!" Neanderthal shouted. "We can win this afternoon!"

"Now what?" I asked Mrs. Dent.

"You've all had your vaccinations?" she asked.

"What's a vac — " Larry started to ask.

"Yes!" Cody shouted, quickly clapping her hand over Larry's mouth.

We hurried into the house and up the stairs to Brian's room. Cody led Larry over to the closet while I closed the bedroom door and made sure Brian sat down at the computer.

"You know what you have to do," I told him.

"Listen," he whispered. "You and I can make a deal. Maybe you won't have any hands, but I promise you'll always get dates."

"Forget it," I said. "Just get Larry, I mean, Abe, back where he belongs."

Brian sighed. "You're making a big mistake, Max." Then he hunched over the computer and started to type. I looked over at Cody and Larry by the closet. They were holding hands. Larry was speaking quietly. Cody sniffed and wiped a tear away from her eye. It would have looked kind of touching if Larry hadn't been wearing makeup and a dress.

"Where do you think *you're* going?" Mrs. Dent's voice echoed up the stairs.

"They've kidnapped my star basketball player!" Neanderthal gasped. "You have to let me in." He must have gotten past Ms. Schmidt.

"Not until you take off your shoes!"

"Are you crazy? Get out of my way!"

"Ooof!" "Uuhhh!" Thud! Crash! The sound of a scuffle followed. Mrs. Dent was taking on Neanderthal. I wished I could see that one!

"Hurry!" I yelled at Brian.

"Okay, okay," Brian said. "I'm going to send him to Illinois. If that's a mistake, it's not my fault."

"Ow!" Thunk! "Yikes!" The sound of the fracas was coming closer.

"Just do it!" I yelled.

"You sure you want him going back dressed like that?" Brian pointed at Larry.

"He'll just have to deal with it," I said.

"Okay," Brian said. "Close the closet door."

I ran over to the closet. Larry and Cody were holding hands and looking longingly into each other's eyes.

"Sorry, guys, time to go," I said.

Cody took a step back, but she wouldn't let go of Larry's hand.

"Stop it!" Wham! "Ouch!" Neanderthal and

Mrs. Dent were in the hallway right outside Brian's room.

"Cody, you have to let go!" I hissed, pulling apart their hands.

"I'll never forget you!" Cody cried.

Bang! Bang! Bang! "Let me in!" Neanderthal was banging on Brian's door.

Larry had a pained look on his face. He stepped back into the closet. I held out my hand.

"You're the bravest person I ever met," I said. "I won't forget you either."

Larry nodded and we shook hands. He practically crushed mine.

"One more step back," I said.

Larry sighed and stepped back. "One small step for man; one giant leap for mankind."

"Don't say that!" Cody gasped.

Larry frowned. "Why not?"

"Because Neil Armstrong used it on the moon," Cody said.

"Well, I'd like to say *something* significant," Larry said.

"Think about government of the people and by the people," Cody suggested.

"Hmmm." Larry nodded. "I'll work on that. Thanks." He waved and I closed the closet door. "Okay, Brian!" I shouted.

Over at the computer, Brian pushed the red button. The closet started to rumble. Vapors and light began to seep through the cracks.

Crash! Neanderthal knocked the door off its hinges and stumbled into the room. He was covered with bruises and scratches. His clothes were tattered. "Where is he?"

We all looked at the closet. Following our eyes, Neanderthal ran over and yanked open the door. The closet was filled with thick glowing vapors.

"Don't!" Brian shouted.

But it was too late. Neanderthal dove into the closet and disappeared.

"Where'd he go?" I gasped, staring at the glowing vapors.

"I don't know," Brian said. "He's in an endless free fall through time."

Now Mrs. Dent staggered into the room. Her hair was a mess and her clothes were askew. "Look at this mess!" she screeched at the broken door. "Where is that awful man?"

Brian pointed at the closet.

"The closet?" Mrs. Dent's jaw dropped. "I just finished cleaning it!"

Before we could stop her, Mrs. Dent rushed into the closet.

"Wait!" Brian shouted.

"Turn off the time machine!" Cody yelled.

Brian quickly hit the red button.

The closet grew still. The vapors and light gradually disappeared.

Then everything got quiet.

The closet was empty. Larry, Coach Neanderthal, and Mrs. Dent were all gone.

Ms. Schmidt staggered into the room. Her clothes were rumpled. "Wha . . . what happened?"

Cody and I looked at Brian. He blinked back a tear.

"They're gone," Cody said.

"All of them?" Ms. Schmidt gasped. "Even Brian's mom?"

We all looked at Brian. He nodded sadly. "I just hope that wherever she's gone, they have vacuum cleaners."

23

We never told anyone what had happened. Ms. Schmidt said it was okay because if we tried to tell anyone, they'd just think we were crazy anyway. After a while, a rumor started going around that Coach Neanderthal and Mrs. Dent ran away with each other. I guess in a way they did.

That afternoon we played our last game. Of course Larry and Coach Neanderthal weren't there, so Mr. Foote coached. Dave played out of his mind and we actually won! For the first time ever, the Putney basketball team finished with a winning season! Coach Neanderthal would have been proud.

Brian's father moved back into the house after that, and Brian continued to come to school. Cody was sad for a couple of months, but then she got better. I found myself thinking about Larry a lot. About the way he was always willing to help, and how he insisted on always telling the truth. About how he never quit trying, and how he went out of his way to help other people solve their problems. In a funny way, I learned a lot from him.

But there was other stuff happening in our lives. After a while we pretty much stopped thinking and talking about it.

Then one day in eleventh grade we went on a field trip to the American History museum. We had started with the beginning of time and were working our way forward. Brian and Ms. Schmidt were there, along with Cody and the rest of the class.

As we walked through the Stone Age section I suddenly froze in front of a large glass display case. Inside was a life-size depiction of a Stone Age family in a cave. Cody stopped and looked back at me. "Max, what is it?"

I couldn't answer. I was totally speechless. Cody walked back and looked at the display case.

"Oh, gosh!" she gasped.

Brian must have noticed something because he came over. "I don't believe it!"

Then Ms. Schmidt joined us. "Unbelievable!"

Inside the display case, a couple of wild-haired kids in animal skins played with some bones. Behind them stood a small cave woman with squinty eyes. She was holding a stick with some twigs tied to it, sort of like a Stone Age broom.

And standing over them all was the father. He had dark hair and a sloping forehead and deep-set eyes. Under one arm he carried a large round rock about the size of a basketball, and the fingers of his other hand were stuck in his mouth as if he were trying to whistle.

"Do you think it's possible?" Cody whispered.

"It's too much of a coincidence *not* to be," Ms. Schmidt said. Just as we had three years before, we all turned to Brian.

"Well," he said with a shrug, "I think she was happy."

"How do you know?" I asked.

"Brian pointed at the display case. "None of them are wearing shoes."

About the Author

Todd Strasser has written many award-winning novels for young and teenage readers. Among his best known are *Please* Don't *Be Mine, Julie Valentine!* and *Help! I'm Trapped in the First Day of School.* His next project for Scholastic will be a series about a dog detective.

Mr. Strasser speaks frequently at schools about the craft of writing and conducts writing workshops for young people. He lives in a suburb of New York City with his wife and children.

GET
Goosebumps™
by R.L. Stine

APPLE® PAPERBACKS

Pick an Apple and Polish Off Some Great Reading!

BEST-SELLING APPLE TITLES

☐ MT43944-8 **Afternoon of the Elves** Janet Taylor Lisle ... $2.75

☐ MT43109-9 **Boys Are Yucko** Anna Grossnickle Hines ... $2.95

☐ MT43473-X **The Broccoli Tapes** Jan Slepian ... $2.95

☐ MT40961-1 **Chocolate Covered Ants** Stephen Manes ... $2.95

☐ MT45436-6 **Cousins** Virginia Hamilton ... $2.95

☐ MT44036-5 **George Washington's Socks** Elvira Woodruff ... $2.95

☐ MT45244-4 **Ghost Cadet** Elaine Marie Alphin ... $2.95

☐ MT44351-8 **Help! I'm a Prisoner in the Library** Eth Clifford ... $2.95

☐ MT43618-X **Me and Katie (The Pest)** Ann M. Martin ... $2.95

☐ MT43030-0 **Shoebag** Mary James ... $2.95

☐ MT46075-7 **Sixth Grade Secrets** Louis Sachar ... $2.95

☐ MT42882-9 **Sixth Grade Sleepover** Eve Bunting ... $2.95

☐ MT41732-0 **Too Many Murphys** Colleen O'Shaughnessy McKenna ... $2.95

Available wherever you buy books, or use this order form.

Scholastic Inc., P.O. Box 7502, 2931 East McCarty Street, Jefferson City, MO 65102

Please send me the books I have checked above. I am enclosing $_____ (please add $2.00 to cover shipping and handling). Send check or money order — no cash or C.O.D.s please.

Name_____ Birthdate_____

Address _____

City_____ State/Zip _____

Please allow four to six weeks for delivery. Offer good in the U.S.A. only. Sorry, mail orders are not available to residents of Canada. Prices subject to change.

APP693